WINTERS' WAR

Eight years after a bloody range war, the Winters family has strived to build up a promising ranch in Wyoming's rugged Rockies. But ahead of the season's first snow-storm a stranger arrives to rip open old wounds. Niall Winters returns from selling his fall herd to find his ranch in ruins, his Uncle Drift dead, and his wife missing. He heads into the storm determined to confront this demon from his past, little knowing the horrors that await him . . .

MATTHEW P. MAYO

88

WINTERS' WAR

Complete and Unabridged

LINFORD
Leicester

First published in Great Britain in 2007 by
Robert Hale Limited
London

First Linford Edition
published 2008
by arrangement with
Robert Hale Limited
London

The moral right of the author has been asserted

British Library CIP Data

Mayo, Matthew P.
    Winters' war.—Large print ed.—
Linford western library
1. Western stories
2. Large type books
I. Title
823.9'2 [F]

ISBN 978–1–84782–472–1 .

Published by
F. A. Thorpe (Publishing)
Anstey, Leicestershire

Set by Words & Graphics Ltd.
Anstey, Leicestershire
Printed and bound in Great Britain by
T. J. International Ltd., Padstow, Cornwall

This book is printed on acid-free paper

For Jennifer

1

The pistol butt crumpled the worn crown of Drift's hat and cracked his head hard enough to drive him to his knees as if sledged. He pitched to his side on the packed dirt and straw of the stable floor. The floor became the ceiling and kept on moving, sliding away from him. Now someone was fooling with him, trying to put their hands over his eyes. Some sort of kids' game. A face appeared, leaned close over his, and just under a broad black hat brim Drift saw the man's eyes. He knew those eyes. But from where? As his vision darkened the answer came to him, too late. And then he knew two things at once: this was no kiddies' game, and he must already be dead because those same eyes belonged to a man long gone from this earth.

★ ★ ★

With a damp rag Jenna wiped the table
and pans from the morning's baking,
humming the one melody she remembered from her Vermont childhood. Her
gran sang whenever she worked in the
tiny farm kitchen where Jenna spent her
summers. Now, busy in her own
kitchen, Jenna understood why. It made
the work lighter and kept a smile on her
face. Outside, the massive, ragged peaks
of the Wyoming Territory's Rockies
seemed a world and a lifetime away
from those low green hills of her
childhood back East. She could never
recall any more of the song other than
the same short phrase, but it was
enough for baking.

Most of the major fall chores were
well underway or already done, and that
meant the ranch was about as ready as
it would ever be for winter. With Niall
returning later today from selling the
fall stock, it would be the perfect
evening for a feast. And Jenna had just

the meal in mind.

She gave the rag a final shake into the long dry sink and, grabbing a lantern and a match, she went out the back door to the root cellar Niall had dug into the hillside behind the house a few years back. It served them well for wintering over produce from their garden and also proved ideal for ageing game.

She held the oil lantern close by her face and stared with satisfaction at the laden hooks and shelves sagging under the weight of a bountiful summer of gardening, one of their best yet. She selected two plump carrots, hesitated, then slid a third from the hanging bunch. She separated two onions from their bunch, chose a half-dozen potatoes, and lifted down the fine fall turkey she'd been ageing since Uncle Drift shot it days before.

She climbed the four steps up to ground level, blew out the lantern, and held her breath in anticipation of the biting wind awaiting her. If Uncle Drift was right, and he was, as he said, about half the time, this cold wind was a calling card for the first sizable snowstorm of the season. She slammed the cellar door and slid the bolts through their catches, wishing she'd remembered her shawl. She hustled across the yard to the back door, arms full, and into the warmth of the kitchen.

As she set the food on the counter she heard the familiar cold-weather squawk of the metal pump handle raising and lowering. It couldn't be Niall. He wasn't due back until nightfall. And where time and Niall Winters were concerned, you could set your watch to the man's intentions. Could be Uncle Drift, though it was too early for him to be drawing water for the stock. The only time he did that chore early was before he headed to town, and he had just taken his monthly town trip last week. She looked through the small window beside the door.

She couldn't see much of the man at

4

the trough except that he had height and was on the lean side. Though not as tall as her husband, he was wide shouldered. He wore a dark, dirty hat with a tall crown, and black, limp clothes. His horse, a blue roan, drank out of the trough beside him.

I'd better be hospitable, she thought, before Uncle Drift comes out of the barn to pepper this stranger with questions. Drift didn't care that it was rude behavior. He'd say that he's naturally curious and too dang old to be polite any more. She reached for the door handle, thought of the increasing wind and cold, and swung her work shawl over her shoulders.

The door opening and closing hadn't stirred the man. She regarded him fully now. He's either deaf or really thirsty. His horse lifted its head and looked at her, water streaming from its mouth, its ears perked forward. She looked beyond the man and horse toward the barn. No sign of Uncle Drift. He'll be cleaning stalls, she thought, and will not

5

yet have seen the visitor.

'Hello there,' she said. No response. 'You have to raise the pump handle extra high so the gasket doesn't catch,' she said, nodding at the pump. He continued drinking, looking up just enough for her to see his unshaven chin. She saw he had dark hair, and he wore it long. She tried again, 'It's something else we've yet to fix, but it gets us by.' She pulled the shawl tighter about her shoulders.

The man dipped the chipped tin cup that was there for all to use right in the horse water and drank again from it. He didn't look back down at the water, but she didn't think he was looking at her.

'You been here long?' she said, an edge to her tone now. Something about him struck her as familiar, and she was irritated that Uncle Drift still hadn't come out of the barn. For that matter, she wished Niall was back already.

'You come a long ways?' she asked, stepping back onto the porch, just under the shadow of the overhang, enough to keep the cold sun out of her eyes. He still didn't look up, didn't say a thing. But he did nod his head once.

Where was Uncle Drift? It was rare that she couldn't at least hear him from the bunkhouse or the corral just beyond it, though only half of it could be seen from where she was standing.

'If you'll excuse me, I have something on the stove,' she motioned behind her toward the door and turned.

He hung the cup on its nail and looked over at her. 'I ain't eaten in days,' he said. His voice was harsh and low, like river sand ground between rocks. He pushed his ragged coat open and slid his thumb behind a worn black gunbelt. With a long, grimy finger he pushed up his hat brim and walked forward, dropping the reins on the edge of the trough where they flopped into the water. He stopped at the bottom of the steps.

His hands were filthy, the nails long and caked with crescents of dirt. She knew she should move. Retreat to the kitchen, bolt the door, and lift down the shotgun. She knew she should do this but she did not move, could not move. She saw his face fully now for the first time as he looked up at her. And she knew she was seeing a ghost.

But no, it couldn't be. 'Uncle Drift!' she shouted, her voice strained, near hysterical. She didn't care. She shouted again and again. The roan nickered, ears perked, and stepped backward a pace from the trough. That was all. No movement or sound from the barn. She looked to the paddock where the horses were kept. Nothing moved there, either.

She stepped backward toward the door, laid her hand on the latch. 'Uncle Drift,' she said, only loud enough for the stranger to hear her. Jenna looked at him. He stared at her and shook his head.

She put a hand to her mouth and fumbled with the door handle. By the time she got inside and had the door pulled shut he was there, just outside. She grabbed at the deadbolt and almost had it slid home when the door opened wide and the stranger stood, framed by daylight, the wind blowing into the kitchen and rustling his coat and the brim of his hat. Her dress flapped against her legs. He moved into the kitchen and shut the door.

'What do you want?' she said, backing to the far wall, edging toward the back door.

'I said I haven't eaten in a while.'

She stopped. Food. Maybe that's all he wants, then he'll leave. He stepped forward and lifted his gaze. There were those eyes again. It couldn't be him, not after all these years. Not after any amount of time. The dead don't come back to life. She edged toward the countertop where she left her kitchen knife by the vegetables.

'Don't,' he said in that dark voice. He pushed the side of his coat back and rested his hand on the hilt of a sheathed long blade meant for hacking. A pistol sat snug in a holster just behind it. He walked to the table and flipped back the towel covering the biscuits she made for supper. He grabbed a handful, stuffed one in his mouth, held it there, and crammed the rest in his coat pockets. He did everything at an unhurried pace. He emptied the contents of the basket into his pockets and chewed the biscuit in his mouth. It was gone in three bites. 'Good biscuit.'

He stepped around the table and stopped in front of her. She was backed up against the cupboards. She pulled her collar and shawl tight around her throat, but could not stop shaking.

He stared at her as if deciding something. She was right. The face, the eyes, even the voice. It's him, come back from the dead. This can't be happening. She shot a look at the door. Where was Niall? He should be here. This couldn't happen again. It was impossible.

His eyes narrowed and he said, 'Let's go,' as if she should have been expecting him all these years. He turned to the stove, put his hands over it. Now was her chance. She groped behind her for the knife. Carrots, an onion, the turkey — where was the knife? She half-turned.

'You lookin' for this?' he said, holding up her knife. She'd left it to dry on the warming shelf to prevent rust. The stranger tossed the knife behind the stove. It clattered in the wood box.

He turned, held out an arm toward the door, and said, 'Let's go.'

She took a step, stopped, and said, 'Where . . . where are you taking me?' but even as she asked she knew. He looked her square in the eye and nodded slowly. She knew.

⋆   ⋆   ⋆

On their way past the trough he grabbed his horse's reins. She saw extra gear lashed securely, just behind the cantle. It was a stout horse, and appeared to be in good flesh.

'To the barn,' he said.

As she drew near the big double

doors she slowed. Uncle Drift. She didn't want to know, couldn't know. It would be too much. He pushed her in the middle of her back with his knuckles. The touch sent a trail of ice up her spine. She stumbled forward and stood in front of the closed doors.

'Open 'em,' he said.

She obeyed and there lay Uncle Drift in the middle of the barn floor, on his back, arched a bit, his boots moving slowly as if he were trying to walk while lying down. He didn't make a sound. His face was gray like old fabric washed too many times. Dirt and straw were gripped in his hands and there were furrows where his fingers had clawed. A puddle of near-black liquid surrounded his head like a halo. Half of his head was smeared with the same. It can't be blood, she thought. It's much too dark, though she knew better. His crumpled hat lay upturned by his head. The two-tined hay fork lay on the floor a few feet away. She ran to him, dropped to her knees, and took his face in her hands. She whispered his name, told him he would be fine, everything would be fine. But he didn't see her. His eyelids flickered and his tongue looked swollen, gray and thick, too thick for his mouth. She kissed his forehead and heard his breath rasping.

'Get up,' the stranger said. For a second she didn't know who he was talking to.

She looked up at him and shouted, 'You did this! You filthy animal. Why?' He just stood there, staring at her.

She rose to her feet, sobbing, not caring now what happened to her. She lunged at him and, so quick she didn't see it happen, he pulled his pistol. 'Saddle that horse. The bay. Now.' He wagged the pistol toward the horse. He didn't seem concerned about any of the goings-on. The bay was hers, Sweet Baby, Niall's present to her for their wedding anniversary six years ago.

She stood still, clenched her teeth, and stared at him. He pulled the hammer back and said, 'Now' as if he

13

were saying, 'Good soup.'

She still didn't move. He stepped forward and put the end of the pistol barrel against her face, right between her eyes. 'Now.'

She closed her eyes and swallowed. She could not stop shaking, but she did what she needed to, going through motions born of repetition. Her entire life she'd been rigging horses to ride. When her horse was saddled, he pointed his pistol at Slate, Niall's big gray.

'Saddle him, too.' She did as told and then he had her fill two gunny sacks with feed corn, tie them off, and hang them from Slate's saddle horn.

Minutes later they were out of the barn and mounting up. He tied her hands together with rough rope, wrapping the wrists until they throbbed, then he tied them to the saddle horn. It hurt but she was beyond caring. Niall was nowhere to be seen. Uncle Drift would soon die without a doctor's attention, and she was being kidnapped by a ghost from a past she thought was long buried. She took a last look in the half-open door at Uncle Drift. He lay in the same position as before. Cold wind sliced across the yard and blew hair across her face.

The past, she decided as they rode out of the yard, never dies.

'Hyah,' said the stranger and spurred his horse forward. Her horse was last in the short line, following Slate, who was tied behind the stranger's horse. They galloped into the high hills beyond the ranch as the first lazy snowflakes drifted down. The snow, she knew, would soon cover everything in sight.

2

Niall Winters closed the throat of his sheepskin coat with a gloved hand and swayed in the seat of the little work wagon, steering Lippy the mule around the same washout he steered around the last time he was in town, must have been two months before. For late September this north wind was coming in hard and carrying that sweet edge to it that could only mean snow, no mistaking it. You could taste it on the air. And though each year he forgot about it as soon as the first serious snow stayed with them, when the wind again carried that distinctive tang back their way each fall, he recalled it as though he'd smelled it only the day before. Nature's warning shot before it laid down that cold, white blanket.

The first snow usually melted off after little more than a few days, but that didn't mean it couldn't cause plenty of trouble if it caught people unawares. As Lippy picked his way up the barren main street of Dibbston, Niall's thoughts turned toward his home and family nearly twenty miles east of town. He'd headed off three days before, leaving Uncle Drift limping from job to job, complaining about everything at once, and all the while knowing that no one was taking him seriously.

They'd taken turns at the forge, working up the crude pin hinges for the barn doors — neither of them being too adept with the forge, knowing just enough to get them by. The place was getting there, but was not yet ready for winter. He knew that Jenna and Uncle Drift would both disagree with him, but there was so much more that wanted doing before snow flew. With luck he'd be back at the ranch by dark. He sighed and guided Lippy to a stop in front of the Dibbs' Mercantile, right behind some sort of caravan. He squinted into the wind and studied the back end of the thing. Ornate carvings graced the wagon's wood, and a flip-down set of three steps, now secured upright with a length of rope, led to a small Dutch door at the back.

Niall pushed the brake in place with his boot and twisted the reins, looping them over the brake handle. From the top step of the store porch he took another look at the strange wagon. Judging from the scrolled woodwork and faded paint, he guessed it had once been as fine as any circus wagon kept in prime condition. But what would an old circus wagon be doing in Dibbston? He walked along the porch, looking at the horse that pulled the wagon. The harness, judging from the quality of the hardware, like the wagon, had once been grand.

The horse itself, if you could call it a horse, was no greater than a large pony, but it had a tremendous mane, the hair of which was nearly two feet long. And from the condition of the coat and the fair covering of flesh on the beast, he could tell it was well cared for. He turned to go and caught sight of the feet of the pony, the hoofs were nearly as big around as Jenna's finest dinner plates and the long, shaggy hair trailed down the legs, spilling over the mammoth hoofs. He raised his eyebrows and gave the small sturdy beast a nod, then he clunked across the porch and entered the warmth of the store.

★　★　★

Dibbs' Mercantile was as welcoming to him today as it had been nearly ten years ago when he first came to town, though back then the town had no name other than 'town', suiting the blunt nature of the few people who chose to settle in this remote region of Wyoming, and the mercantile had been nothing more than a canvas wall tent. Now, though, the town had grown to include a saloon with rooms above for rent, a livery and blacksmith, an eating house, Dibbs' store, and a handful of homes, sheds, and outbuildings in varying degrees of upkeep.

The store inside felt cozy, packed as it was with merchandise — tack hung from the rafters, boxes and barrels of flour, salt, and other bulk sundries leaned in piles about the room, and lining every wall, displays of canned goods and blankets and weapons. In the middle of it all sat the small stove that today gave off waves of welcoming heat. Niall pushed the door closed and unbuttoned his coat.

'Well hello, Mr Winters,' said a pudding of a man in apron and braces. He had a bald head, long, drooping moustaches, and bushy sideburns like squirrel tails running down his cheeks. 'Suppose we should blame you for this namesake weather of yours.' Aside from his Uncle Drift, Niall had known Bertram Dibbs, along with his wife Esther, about as long and as well as he'd known anybody in his life.

Before Niall could answer, a small

woman, as amply proportioned as Bertram, pierced the air of the room with a scolding tone. 'When are you going to stop calling Niall by his surname? You've known him for a coon's age.' Esther, wife of Bertram, and co-owner of Dibbs' Mercantile, stomped around the counter. Niall had to bend low for the proffered hug.

'When you stop asking me that very question,' said Bertram, winking at Niall. With the slightest of variations, this exchange always greeted him and never failed to hang a smile on his otherwise unreadable face. Esther stepped back and tilted her head to one side. 'Niall, dear. Good to see you.'

'How are you, Bert, Esther?' said Niall, nodding at each in turn and plopping his hat on the seldom used candy end of the long, polished counter.

'I swear,' said Esther, smiling at him. 'We've seen more of the Winters family this month alone than we've seen all summer long. Why, your dear bride Jenna was in just last week picking up her special ord — '

'Esther!' Bert glared at her. She clamped her mouth shut tight and turned her attention to refolding a length of flowered cloth.

'Extra flour's all it was,' said Bert, 'and cornmeal, too, I think. Yep.'

Niall just nodded. Of course, when Jenna told him last week she needed to go back to town so soon after her last visit, he'd suspected it was for more than just the 'stocking up' she said she needed to do before winter set in. Their wedding anniversary was less than a month away, on 23 October, and they both always went out of their way to make it a special day for each other. It had taken on more importance to them, and to Drift, too, oddly enough, than almost any other day of the year.

'See the wagon?' Bert whispered, leaning over the counter toward him.

'Yeah, I was about to ask.'

Bert raised his head and looked over

Niall's shoulder toward the back of the store. Niall leaned on the counter and turned as if to look around the place. A small man, a foot shorter than Niall's six-foot-two-inch frame, thumbed the edges of a pile of blankets, pulling out the paper price tags Esther had pinned to them, then flipping them away as if they were stinging bees. Each time he'd shake his head. Niall was dismayed with himself for not noticing the man right away. But then he had been waylaid by the Dibbses.

The stranger wore a small felt hat that might have been green at one time, but now was dulled and thin along the creases. A limp, black-barred feather drooped from the band. He was dressed in equally worn black wool pants and shirt, this topped by an embroidered wool vest that, like the wagon outside, Niall guessed, had once been colorful. But the most curious thing about him was his feet. They were bare like a boy's in summer and one-quarter his age. The man's feet were hardened, to be sure, and had obviously seen many miles without the benefit of footwear, but it wasn't summer anymore. Wyoming was heading into a time of year when a man took whatever he could to cover himself up in anticipation of harsh treatment from the elements. Esther watched every move the man made, her lips pursed.

'Gypsies,' said Bert, none too quietly, behind Niall's ear.

The small man spun around and stared at them both. Niall saw a swarthy man with a thick, full moustache and the bristling of one who is more accustomed to being clean-shaven. The moustache and whiskers were flecked with gray and Niall guessed that a life full of hard work lined this man's face prematurely. But it was the man's dark, steady eyes, like a mountain ram's, locked on his, that surprised Niall the most.

'We're not gypsies. We're Basque,' said the little man in angular English. 'And we have as much right to be here as any of you.' He spat the words as a challenge, and he squared off, facing Niall, his hands on his hips. He wore no guns. A long skinning knife in a woven sheath hung loose to one side from his belt. His was a stance of defiance. A show of pride, nothing more or less, Niall decided. He had seen it many times in the past and he guessed that he, too, had assumed it at times. In his mind, pride in himself was the first, last, and best thing a man could have.

'Aw, now look here,' said Bert, holding his hands up as if to quiet a noisy room. Before he could say more, the door opened. A stiff, chilling gust whipped in and through the potbelly stove's cracked front grate, fanning the flames to a roar.

'Greasy!' Bert yelled. 'Shut that door! By God, man, how many times today alone have I told you?'

A thin, dirty-faced man in patched buckskins and what was left of a rimless bowler hat took his time in carefully clicking the door closed. He stood, swaying a bit, thumbs hooked in a ragged belt cinching his middle, and regarded the people in the room, each in turn, with two close-set eyes peering out through a tangle of dirty hair. He smiled at them and a mouthful of broken and stained teeth showed through the crack in the matted beard.

'Well now, Winters, I thought that was your nag out there. Times ain't so good when a man as high-falutin' as yourself takes to drivin' a mule.' He held his hands over the stove, almost touching the steel lid.

Niall offered less than a nod, and said, 'Greasy.'

'Greasy, get away from that stove. The heat's driving unspeakable smells off you and I will not have my customers tearing up on account of it.' Esther stared at the skinny swaying man and leaned heavily on the counter as if she might vault it. Greasy tucked his thumbs behind his belt and stepped back from the stove a couple of paces.

The small, barefooted stranger resumed

thumbing through the blankets, and Esther said, 'Mister, are you interested in buying a blanket or just warming your thumb on them? You keep it up you're going to wear them out.'

'Now, Esther,' said Bert, looking up from showing Niall the latest newspaper from Big Pine.

'Don't 'Now Esther' me. I'll — '

'Whew! I thought I smelt sheep. Or worse. Only thing worse than a sheep's a goat, and only thing worse'n a goat's a sheep. 'Cept for a man what'll keep 'em.' Greasy made his way over to the little man.

'Now that is enough, Greasy,' said Bert. 'What do you want, anyway? I dare you to tell me you came in here to spend all your hard-earned money.'

Despite himself Niall chuckled along with Bert and Esther. Greasy's slow decline in the community was by now nothing more than a sad joke. He had come to town as a young man eager to help in the range war eight years back and had stayed, slumping into the

27

unsavory role of town drunk. Since then the liquor aged him prematurely and he made everyone's life a bit uncomfortable. Along with his increasing addiction to booze came a rise in petty crimes in town. Small items and foodstuffs had turned up missing all over Dibbston. Though no one could ever quite catch him in the act, it was generally assumed he was the culprit.

Greasy never spent any more time than was absolutely necessary in working. Cornell Waite, the saloon owner, let him sweep up and empty spittoons, help with odd jobs about the place. And in return he gave Greasy use of an old modified chicken coop to sleep in, plus one meal a day. That Greasy was perpetually tipsy led to the speculation that Waite, always too kind a soul, looked the other way when Greasy nipped from near empties and probably even the inventory.

Niall couldn't be sure, but he might have seen something akin to a blush spread underneath Greasy's hairy face.

The skinny rogue slammed the door on his way out. With the noise, Niall straightened and said, 'Well, I better get cracking, too. Plenty to do before I head home.'

'Are you still a cattle baron?' said Esther.

'We kept just the young stock and some breeders. Sold the rest off. In fact, I'm just back from settling up. But that still leaves us with not a few mouths to feed. I'll need to check on them before I head home.' He nodded toward the door and said, 'Especially with this weather comin' in.' He tossed the list on the counter in front of Bert and said, 'This should do us for a good little while.'

'Lot of heavy items here,' said Bert, eyeing the list through the half-moon spectacles pinching the end of his nose. 'You bring your wagon?'

'Yep, Lippy's — '

A woman's scream from outside reached them. Niall made for the door but the little swarthy stranger pushed past, knocking Niall into a rack of buckets and coils of rope. The man was out the door in an instant with Niall close behind.

The small man was off the steps in two bounds and stood, fists raised, between Greasy and the rear of his own wagon. The door was open and a small woman stood just inside, clutching a shawl tight under her chin. From within the wagon, a dog barked. The man spoke to the woman in an urgent tone over his shoulder, but in a language Niall had never heard. She shook her head, looking down. He said something else and she retreated into the dark wagon, pulling the door shut behind her. In a moment more, the barking ceased. The man turned and faced Greasy, advancing on him.

Greasy stepped backward and bumped into Lippy the mule, who put his head down and butted the skinny man in the back.

'You dare to enter my home, touch my wife! You dare!' Niall never would have guessed the little man could have moved so quick. But in a flash he lunged at Greasy and slapped the shaggy head with the back of his compact, slablike hands so hard that Greasy's head whipped back and forth once, twice before he raised his own hands in a feeble attempt to block the onslaught.

'Winters!' yelled Greasy between slaps. 'Stop him, damn you!' By tossing his head to each side, Lippy kept Greasy from moving too far away from the man's stinging slaps.

'Why should I? Seems like Lip and this gentleman here are doing everything I'd be doing anyway.'

'You take their word over mine?' said Greasy, ducking the blows. 'Them gyps ain't nothing but lyin', sheepherdin' thieves.'

Niall's smile faded. 'That's enough of that talk!' said Niall, who flew off the last step.

'You a gyp lover, Winters?' said Greasy. Niall punched him in the

31

mouth. Greasy stumbled and rolled out into the street.

'Gyp lover!' he said from the ground. He touched his lip and looked at his bloody fingertips. 'Mark my words! Bad things gonna happen to you!'

The barefoot man followed, pushing him down with a kick from a calloused foot every time Greasy tried to rise. Eventually Greasy made it to the far side of the street. He crawled up the steps of the saloon, just below a few men who'd come out in time to see about the commotion.

Their presence emboldened Greasy, who pointed at the small stranger in the middle of the street, his hands unclenched and hanging at his sides, his chest heaving.

'No call, he ain't had no call to go whompin' on me!' He turned to the men on the step above him and pointed, saying, 'Gypsies! Stinkin' gypsies!' as if a tornado was bearing down on them. He turned back, still pointing at them all, the little swarthy man, at

Niall and the Dibbses on the steps of the mercantile, and said, 'You mark my words, ain't nothing good ever follows one of them around. Nothing but misery, I tell you. Stinkin' misery. Bad things gonna happen to you, Winters! You don't know the half of it!'

Greasy stared at Niall, shaking his head and laughing until he coughed, then he pushed his way past his audience and into the saloon.

★   ★   ★

The man walked back to his wagon, and Niall said, 'Don't pay him any mind. He's a drunken bum.'

The man stared at him, those hard eyes not softening one bit. Niall shrugged and headed back up the steps as the man and his wife whispered low in their foreign tongue. The man helped the woman mount the wagon seat up front. As she climbed up Niall couldn't help but notice that under her long skirt she was wearing what must have been an extra pair of her husband's pants, and her feet were covered with several layers of socks, each showing another through holes. She spread a thin blanket on her lap, leaving enough to cover her husband's legs. As he unstrapped the pony from the rail Niall walked down the steps, even with him.

'You needed something from inside,' he said, gesturing over his shoulder. 'Maybe I can help?' He smiled, trying to soften the obvious blow this would cause to the man's pride.

The man faced Niall. Those dark eyes stared hard back at him and when he spoke it was in a controlled voice on the edge of snapping, each word clipped and distinct. 'We want nothing from anyone here. Leave us alone.'

Niall sighed. He had heard enough. Coming storm or no, a man that proud would never accept help. But then the small woman on the wagon spoke. Her voice was strong, but hesitant. 'We need blankets — '

'No!' said her husband, shaking his

head, anger creasing his swarthy features. He climbed up beside her and scowled at her before gathering the reins.

Niall wrestled with his thoughts and all he could hear was Jenna saying how he should have kept trying. That was her to a T. Keep on trying. He sighed and stepped down in front of the little horse, saying, 'Whoa, whoa,' and kept a hand on it as he walked around to the man's side of the wagon. He saw the muscles in the man's jaw flexing as if working on tough steak.

He raised a hand and said, 'Now, now just hear me out. I know you're not from around here.' He gestured toward the man's bare feet with his chin and said, 'I don't make it a habit to pry into a man's business, but you need a sight more than blankets, if you'll pardon me for noticing.' Beneath his whiskers and thick moustache, the man's face worked up to a new shade of red, so Niall spoke fast. 'If you head on out of town in the direction you're headed, in about two hours, I'd say with this rig, you'll come to my place. Can't miss it. Couple of cabins, barn, and a low, one-storey house. My wife, Jenna, will be there. Tell her Niall sent you, that's me. Niall Winters. My Uncle Drift is there, too. Our bunkhouse is empty, perfect place for you to ride out the storm.'

From the stony stare the man directed at the distance in front of him and the thankful but defeated look the woman offered to Niall, he knew it was a lost cause. But the man hadn't yet strapped the pony into motion, so Niall continued.

'Look, mister. Look at me.' The man stared down at him, his rage replaced by a look of bare tolerance.

'Now I know what a man's pride means, believe me. But this is a snow wind. I can smell it. And what's more I've got a few spots on my body where I can feel it. First storm of the season. Probably won't amount to much, but sometimes you just can't tell. Could be a doozy. It'd be better if you hole up somewhere, let it blow over, then head on your way. And for your sake I hope that way is south of here. But right now, you haven't got much choice. Go to my place. We have plenty of room for you two and your horse.'

Just then the dog's muffled bark sounded from the wagon. 'And your dog,' said Niall, smiling. 'All right?' Niall waited for the man to nod, but he just stared straight ahead. Niall looked at the woman. She nodded and smiled. He couldn't be sure but he thought maybe she looked a little more hopeful. Well, he thought, if that's all I did, at least it was something.

The little man, who suddenly looked older than he had just minutes before, made a clicking sound with his mouth and snapped the reins. The pony stepped into it and the wagon lurched forward. Niall stepped back and, as they passed, he raised his voice, 'You'd be doing me a favor if you'd tell my wife I'll be along soon.'

3

Since leaving the ranch, the stranger stopped now and again with no warning and, leaning from the saddle, hacked sloppy hunks out of saplings and grown trees with his machete. Then he'd lean back, stare at the mess he'd created, and sheath the big knife before spurring the roan into a trot. He wanted Niall to follow, that much was obvious to Jenna.

He seemed to know where he was headed, though Jenna lost count of how many times he stopped and peered through the thickening snow at the surrounding foothills. This time they reined in by a massive gray boulder covered with lichen. He looked down for a moment as if consulting a map, though there was nothing in his lap or in his hands. Jenna knew it was mostly the north side of trees and rocks that lichen grew on, something Uncle Drift had taught her. At the sudden thought of him her throat tightened and she squeezed her eyes tight, fighting tears, refusing to cry in front of this vicious man.

If I want to get out of this alive, she thought, then I'd better do something. But what? Niall always says that doing anything is better than nothing. Maybe if I can get the stranger to talk. She swallowed and cleared her throat. 'Have you been here before?'

He didn't look up, didn't flinch, but said, after a moment, 'Just you never mind.'

It was the most he'd said since they left the ranch. The deepness of his voice still startled her, not that she'd heard much of it. But it came out harsh for a man still too young to have acquired the layered muscle and girth of a man heading into his middle years. Certainly his stature was nothing compared to Niall's solid frame.

She'd teased Niall in bed the winter before about the beginnings of a belly he had forming. She'd patted it and said it wouldn't be long before she'd have to make him new pants. He laughed with her but she noticed his second helpings at dinner were less frequent and she'd not teased him like that again. She felt bad about forgetting that their difference in ages bothered him. That she was nine years his junior was and would always be a sensitive topic to him.

'Wake up.'

His voice was like a slap that pulled her from her reverie.

'I wasn't sleeping,' she snapped, but all she got in response was the back of his coat as he spurred his horse onward into the darkening day, the slack in the lead line jerking Sweet Baby's head up and pulling her into a trot. Jenna gripped the pommel and struggled to stay upright in the saddle. If she fell she might break an arm or worse, be dragged. She had a feeling he wouldn't stop for much.

Jenna had plenty of time to work on

freeing herself from the rope binding her hands to the saddle but he had tied it too well, the knots of someone who didn't like surprises. Her uncovered hands were chafed raw about the wrists from the rough hemp. The blood was cut off and the air so cold she could no longer feel anything more than a dull, throbbing ache below her elbows.

The wind and snow increased throughout the afternoon and by twilight it buffeted them from all sides, curling in through the trees and slicing at them as they ascended the foothills that led to Shiller's Peak. Back at the ranch she guessed where they were headed, but that was a guess based on fear. It couldn't be there that he was taking her, it was just not possible.

She had only her shawl about her shoulders, but was thankful that she had taken to wearing her one-piece long underwear under her dress days ago when the cold snap kicked in. Still, it wasn't enough to keep her entirely warm. Already her face was numb and she couldn't feel her ears.

Ten minutes after they left the big gray rock behind the wind increased in intensity and she was racked with bouts of uncontrollable shivering. The temperature must have dropped twenty degrees since they left the ranch behind. 'I need a blanket,' she shouted at the broad coat twenty feet ahead. No response. She shouted again, her entire body shaking so hard she was afraid she might fall from the horse and he would never know. She could be dragged for miles and he might never turn around. 'Hey!' she shouted. He spurred the horse as it slowed in the day's waning light, picking its way through the evergreens.

She hadn't been this far up into the mountains in eight years. Not since the range war. Not since — but it couldn't be that. Yes it could, she told herself. Don't be so surprised. You knew from the moment you saw his eyes who he was. He's come back to finish what he started so long ago. And this time there's no stopping him because this time he's a ghost. This time he's already dead. A shiver racked her body. But it wasn't from the cold.

4

Niall watched the colorful little wagon roll away, clunking through muddied ruts in the stiffening main street. As he turned to go back into the store he caught sight of Greasy's face peering through the glass of the saloon door. Greasy raised his mug and grinned at him.

Niall turned away, shaking his head and walking up the steps to the store. He knew the Dibbses were just inside, staring out through the door, watching everything. And hearing it, too. Good people, but unlike most folks in these parts they were inclined to be a little nosy. And probably too wary of strangers and quick to forget that they, too, had been strangers to these hills not long ago. Their advantage, unlike the strangers who just left, lay in the fact that they didn't look much different than most of the other folks who lived in these parts.

He closed the door behind him, the bell clanged briefly. The Dibbses both looked up from their work as if surprised to see him. Bert came out from behind the counter and poured two mugs of coffee from the tin pot on the little woodstove and handed one to Niall. They each sipped, then Bert said, 'Greasy's not wholly wrong, you know, Niall.'

Niall said nothing. Bert resumed filling his order, stuffing it into gunny sacks and wooden crates. 'Oh he's a scoundrel all right. But in this instance, I'll say he's not wrong. What I heard of gypsies, they're takers.'

'The man said they aren't gypsies. You heard him as well as I did.'

'Oh now, Niall, don't be sore with me. But you're splitting hairs here. This, that, the other . . . all the same in my book. You can bet he's the scout party, up here looking for land to graze his sheep on.' He wagged a little brown-paper parcel at Niall and said, 'And that's the last thing we need in this part of the country.'

'Since when did you become an authority on livestock, Dibbs?' said his wife. 'You couldn't even manage to feed that mouser we had when I visited my sister last year.'

All three were quiet for a moment. Niall sipped his coffee and regarded them through the steam. Good folks, he knew, but in this instance Bert was wrong. He also knew it wouldn't do to start a gripe with friends. Agree to disagree, that's what Uncle Drift always says. But he just couldn't help himself. 'I didn't see any sheep.'

'Well, no,' resumed Bert, as if there had been no interruption. Niall had to smile. 'But where's there's a gyp, there's bound to be sheep. Come spring we'll be crawling with 'em, sure as mites on a mule. No offense to Lippy.'

'That should tickle you. More business.'

'Oh, this town sees plenty of folks,'

said Bert, running a stubby finger down Niall's list.

Niall looked around. 'Doesn't exactly look like they're bustin' down your door, now Bert.' Niall caught Esther's eye and winked.

'It's just that nobody stops long enough to spend any money,' she said, smiling.

'Plenty of strangers, though,' said Bert. 'We had them gypsies, and there was that other fella yesterday.'

'Who was that?' said Niall, warming his hands over the stove.

'Dunno. Didn't see him myself, Greasy said he was just someone blowin' through.'

'Well he picked a fine time to do that. Speakin' of blowing through, I better get going. I have to check on the last of my herd before I can head home tonight.'

'What can you do with 'em anyway?' said Bert, pushing the last bulging sack down the counter.

'With what?' said Niall.

'Why, sheep, of course,' said Bert, looking at Niall as if he had just broken into song.

'Oh, I don't know,' said Esther. 'Might be nice to have some local wool for spinning. It's so expensive to have it brought in. And I know someone who's going to have a need for wool soon — what with her new wheel and all.'

Niall set down the crate he'd just hefted off the counter. 'Speaking of that, do you know when it will arrive?'

'Oh my word, I can't believe I forgot to tell you.' She cursed herself as she headed into the back stockroom, muttering the entire way. Bert just shook his head.

'You come back here, Bert, and lend me a hand,' she yelled. Bert hustled to the back room and in a minute they emerged carrying a small wooden crate, nearly three feet square and a foot tall. 'I expect you'll have to assemble it some, Niall,' said Bert, huffing as they set it on the counter.

'You don't say,' said Esther, rolling

her eyes at Niall. 'Now I didn't open it, but it's probably packed well. I expect it'll all be there.'

'That didn't take long,' said Niall, staring at the crate that housed his wife's anniversary present.

'Less than a month,' she said, nodding as if she had driven the stage all the way from Big Pine, three days' hard ride.

'I thought I'd ordered it too late.' Niall drummed his fingers on the box. 'Jenna's going to be so pleased.'

'You folks have a lot to be thankful for, especially considering how close you came to losing her in that range war — ' Bert caught his wife's look and stopped talking.

They all stared at the crate for a few seconds, not saying anything. Then Niall said, 'Well, I really got to go now or I'll never get home tonight.' He pulled out his money pouch and settled up with Esther. It was always a wordless exchange of money with the Dibbses, as if it was something they'd rather not discuss.

Minutes later, with the wagon loaded and Lippy watered, they started down the street. Niall waved to his friends, then cut a brisk pace in the same direction the painted wagon took a half-hour earlier. It was past midday. Just enough time to check on the last of the herd. Afterward he would still have a good few hours of useful light left before he had to find the road again and head home.

From their porch Esther watched the little work wagon jostle and clunk around the muddied rust at the far end of Main Street. Then she slapped Bert on the arm and said, 'Fool.'

'What are you on about?'

'Ever think they might just want to forget about the past and work on building a future together? You bringing up that damn range war all the time sure don't let things heal.' She shook her head and went inside. Bert watched until Niall's wagon was long out of sight.

5

There is no way I'm going to let them get away with that, thought Greasy. Everybody knows that gypsies all hoard the gold and riches they steal from people and I'm gonna get me some. It's there for the plucking.

Beer in hand, courtesy of one of the boys who had no particular love of anybody who didn't speak English right enough for his tastes, Greasy had watched the little faded wagon rattle and sway, headed east down Main Street, with the old couple in the seat, acting all high and mighty. But seeing Winters staring back at him through the window brought the stranger from the day before back to mind.

He had been a quiet sort and none too friendly. Seemed like the man was waitin' on him. Nobody else interested him, just Greasy. Offered his hand to the man and said, 'They call me Greasy.' The man nodded, as if he'd known who Greasy was. Then he invited Greasy to the end of the bar. Said he just wanted to know where Niall Winters lived. Greasy offered to take him to Winters, but he said no, he'd find it alone. Greasy hadn't been out Winters' way in months.

He was a piece of work, was that stranger. Curious without asking much. But his money was good and he'd seen Greasy as the only one in the place who could help him. That meant the stranger was smart, at any rate. Greasy had to do most of the talking. Asked a lot about that range war. Winters come out of it okay? That seemed all he was interested in. Winters this, Winters that. Why you wanna know that? Greasy had asked. That's old news, mister.

But he just finished his whiskey, that was it. He turned to go, stopped, and turned around. 'I'll be comin' back this way. Be better if no one gets curious about our talk. Wanna surprise old Niall

Winters. It's been a long time.' He'd pulled out five dollars in coins and stacked them in front of Greasy on the counter. 'More where that came from.' He turned to go, then looked over his shoulder, 'For quiet people, anyway.' Then he just headed on out of town in the direction of Winters' place and that was it. Funny thing was, the only thing Greasy could remember clearly about the man was his eyes. They were hidden most of the time under that big hat pulled low, but at the end when he spoke of money, those eyes fixed on Greasy and he'd had to look away. They were too cold and empty to suit Greasy.

That five dollars lasted Greasy exactly one hour. He reacquainted himself with quite a few old friends and before he knew it he was halfway to drunk and fully broke and friendless again. He passed the rest of the day the same as he always did, sweeping out the bar, bottle-brushing empties, and dumping spittoons. But he gave thought to that strange fellow, convinced he was after something more than meeting up with an old friend.

Come to think of it, he wasn't even sure that fellow was an old friend of Winters. Winters didn't have many friends that Greasy could tell. Winters' whole clan was a quiet bunch, pretty much kept to themselves, even Drift when he came to town. So what was this fellow up to?

The next day when Winters came riding in on that wagon with his damn mule, Greasy had decided to ask Niall what a little information about a certain stranger might be worth to him. Then Winters defended those damn gypsies and that tore it for Greasy. He decided then and there to hell with this town. Them gyps had a fortune in gold just waiting for the right person to come along and help themselves to it. If it wasn't him, it would be someone else down the road.

That would take care of that smug rancher, too. Lie down with dogs, you get fleas, that's what his mother always said. Well they must be hopping all over

Winters, the way he took sides with them gyps. And when he was finished with the gyps, maybe he'd play that stranger for a little more than five dollars. If there was more where that came from, by God, then he would have it. Then he'd set to work on Niall Winters. Finally have something to lord over that smug rancher. And that was a good feeling. The stranger would have to bring on the cash or Greasy would go to Winters and tip him off, though not before he got a little something for his troubles. For the first time in a long time, Greasy felt the warmth of power seep into his skinny frame. And he liked it just fine.

★   ★   ★

Bolstered by the beer and still filled with venom over the beating he'd taken at the hands of Niall and that damn gyp, Greasy made his decision. He guessed the gyps were headed toward Big Pine, so he'd start with them before they got too far out of range. Then, since he knew where the stranger was headed, Greasy figured he'd head off toward Winters' place, maybe even before Winters himself got there.

This is my one big chance, he thought. Then I can take that money and go somewhere south, find a town, maybe do a little gambling, get a woman. A fresh start. Could be good for me, he thought. Could be real good.

He gulped the last swallow in his mug, slammed it down on the bar, and headed out the back door, through the storage room. As he passed all those bottles, the last row full, just out of reach, he remembered what Cornell had told him. Said he'd put up with an awful lot but not the theft of any full bottles. Greasy knew what he meant, of course, and he'd been careful to avoid it whenever he couldn't cover his tracks right, but now things were different. They weren't going to laugh at him anymore because he just wouldn't be around.

With a last look at the closed door that led to the bar, he reached high up over the rows of empty bottles and grasped the neck of a full soldier. He lifted it free and stuffed it into his coat. 'For the journey,' he said in a low voice, and slipped out the back door. He retrieved his bony nag from the little plot Waite let him have to picket the beast, and slapped his old saddle on the horse, which didn't seem to care one way or another.

'Should've sold you when you still had ambition and flesh,' said Greasy, though he knew if he had he'd be walking today.

He had nothing of value in the little converted, coop where he slept in the warmer weather, the bar-room floor in the winter, so he just mounted up. Cradling the weight of the full bottle with one arm he kicked at the horse until it carried him east, behind the little row of buildings that formed the rest of Main Street, and he headed out of town.

He had to time this right, go too fast and he'd come upon the gypsies too soon. Too slow and Winters might catch up with him, even if he was just driving an old mule. As soon as the road curved left into the trees less than a quarter-mile past town he pulled the cork and upended the bottle. The burning wash in his mouth and throat felt good, except for what was left of those few bottom teeth. They throbbed something awful and he knew from experience that they would do so until he could numb them in good shape.

'We get to them gypsies and we'll get you some corn, horse. Bound to have something to feed that show pony of theirs.' He regarded the bony head of his nag and said, 'Can't you move any faster? I seen dead horses on a battlefield put more effort into what they was doin' than you.'

He swallowed more whiskey and, despite the wind that kicked up even harder since daybreak, he found he didn't mind it so much. In fact, he was sure that the wind forced the whiskey to work harder, keeping him warmer than he would have been even if he had a proper winter coat and gloves. Still, he thought, he wished he had a proper winter coat and gloves like Winters. Should have everything he has, thought Greasy. He snorted and took another pull on the bottle. Just by luck that he got it all while I got nothing, had to work all these years just to get by while he rides around in a wagon with his mule, then goes home to that pretty little thing in her tight dresses looking like she just can't wait to get herself out of 'em.

Greasy sucked at the bottle and swallowed hard until it was gone. He sneered at the empty vessel, thinking he should have taken two, and dug his heels into the horse's sides. As they passed a large boulder he threw the bottle hard. It skinned off the side and into the bushes. He gritted the teeth on the right side of his mouth — teeth were more plentiful on that side — and considered turning back to find the bottle to enjoy the satisfaction of truly smashing it, but the nag was still moving at a steady clip and he thought it best to not interrupt her.

He hadn't been out this way in months. Maybe he should just pay a visit to old Drift. He was always good for a drink when Winters and that little prude of a wife of his let him off the ranch once a month to come into town. The old dog probably had a bottle hidden away somewhere on the place. He was sure the turnoff to Winters' spread was just ahead another few miles. He could head on in there, spend some time with Drift, maybe get some home cookin' from Winters' woman — despite her hoity-toity attitude, she was a fair hand in the kitchen — then retrace and catch up with the gypsies. They would most certainly stop at night to camp, and since he was an experienced tracker, he could keep going in the dark and catch up with them. He smiled and urged the now flagging horse into another short-lived trot.

★   ★   ★

A slicing gust of wind whipped off Greasy's hat and he awoke as the cold worked its fingers through his matted, thinning hair. He was still in the saddle but the horse was standing motionless in the road, hunched and head bowed. The wind came from behind them. He rubbed his face with his hands and looked for signs of anyone else. It took almost a full minute before he could call to mind the reasons for him being there. And here happened to be a fork in the road.

Straight on, the road wound east around the looming mountain range. It would eventually take him to Big Pine. To his right lay the branch of road, smaller than the other, that angled south-east, to Winters' ranch. He must have dozed off and the horse, with no urging, had simply stopped walking and instead huddled against the increasing wind.

Greasy knew he slept a good little while. 'Like Mother used to say, 'You wouldn't have slept if you didn't need to'.' He saw his hat pinned in roadside brush. He had a devil of a time getting down, making his way to the hat, and getting back on the horse. That's what a bottle of whiskey on the inside will do to you, he thought, pleased that he was beginning to warm up again from the exertion. The snow had begun to accumulate in little clumps off to the side of the road where the wind couldn't push it away.

He was about to continue east and skip Winters' altogether, considering the time he lost to snoozing, when thoughts of Drift's whiskey and hot food helped his arms rein that horse to the right. He could always catch up with the slow-moving gyps. They were old and riding a box with wheels pulled by a pony, whereas he was a lone man astride a fleet horse.

All along the road from town he'd seen sign of the gypsy wagon. The wheel ruts were one thing, but here and there where the road was low and the recent rain left the ground soft, he'd seen hoofprints as big around as a man's head. Maybe bigger. No other beast in these parts other than that gypsy pony could leave such a mark. Maybe a plowhorse, but he hadn't seen many of them in town lately. No, he was confident those gyps were heading east around the mountains toward Big Pine. And he saw no sign of them turning into Winters' road. He pulled his head down into his ragged coat, mashed his old bowler tight to his eyebrows, and nudged the horse in the ribs, but it held its pace, trudging up the gradual incline toward Winters' ranch.

*   *   *

As he and the horse emerged from the trees Greasy knew that something was wrong. And he knew what it was. The nosy stranger had paid the Winters a visit. But Greasy knew that Winters himself wasn't home. Greasy stopped the horse and sat there for a full minute, looking across the meadow to his right at the low ranch home with the deep porch. Oddest of all, considering this wind and snow, the door was open and the chimney wasn't offering much smoke. Chickens were out, doing whatever it was that chickens found so fascinating to do all day long in the dirt. Between the house and corral Greasy saw the curve of the old road winding out of the yard and leading to the craggy foothills that formed the base of this dwindling arm of the Rockies.

The barn and bunkhouse beyond, tucked to the left, also looked odd. Something not quite right hung in the air. One big door lay flopped open and he thought he heard a calf bleating somewhere off behind the barn. Probably needed feeding. He hated that noise. Grew up on a farm and could never get used to the sound of a crying baby of any breed, be they people or pigs or cattle. It was like ice water dumped on his head every time he heard it.

He slapped the horse on the rump and they headed to the barn. When he got within twenty feet he yelled, 'Drift? Drift, it's me. Greasy. You around? I come to visit.'

Though he didn't expect a reply, he was still shocked that the old man's voice hadn't shot out at him from the back of the barn, asking him what in heck he wanted. He dismounted and left the reins to drag in the dirt. The horse hunched up against the wind. He peeked inside the barn but there was no one there. It was late afternoon and the sun would be heading down soon. He leaned his head in deeper and shouted. 'Drift? You in here? I come for a drink. Say howdy.'

A blink of movement in the dark to his left was all the warning he got before something rapped the side of his head. He dropped to his knees and fell to the dirt, holding his hands over his head. 'Don't kill me!' he shouted.

The only sound, other than the wind outside, was heavy breathing that he figured was not the same as his own heavy breathing, and then there was an odd scuffing noise. Whoever it was now stood right beside him, probably over him. That stranger from town. That's who it was. Had to be. Drift knew Greasy, it wouldn't be him. And Winters wasn't home yet. And his wife, well, he hoped she was just too lady-like to be hitting people in the head like that. He decided, as he crouched there, his face hidden against the stable floor, to roll as fast as he could to his left and away from the attacker.

He rolled and, as he came out of it he yelled and much to his surprise he sprang to his feet with the agility of a Greasy long-since past. But even more surprising was the fact that a spooky, phantom version of Drift stood there, leaning against nothing, but leaning just the same, holding a hay fork and breathing hard.

'Drift? That you? What are you doing attacking me?' He rubbed his head and stared at the old man. Something was wrong with him but he did not know just what. And then he saw Drift's head. Half of his face, partially hidden by the afternoon's lengthening shadows, was darkened. Blood maybe?

The old man gave a yell and a lunge. 'You!'

Greasy jumped to the side and said, 'I don't know nothing about this but you got me wrong, Drift.'

The old man roared again and lunged, with the fork aimed right at Greasy. He stepped to the side, grabbed at the fork, and wrenched it free from Drift's hands. Drift staggered, bellowing nonsense like a shot bear, and finally focused on Greasy again. 'You!' he shouted, his voice a slurred smear.

'Drift! It's me. Greasy. Now calm down!' Greasy held the fork in front of him, the two tines poised like a giant skeletal hand. Drift staggered forward, swinging his arms like clubs and saying, 'You! You did this!'

Greasy backed up until he felt the end of the fork handle clunk against the far closed door. Drift lunged again and Greasy watched as the two tines of the fork sank into the old man's chest. A thin hiss like escaping steam left Drift's mouth and pushed into Greasy's face. He and Drift stared at each other, their faces inches apart.

The old man's eyes kept opening and shutting, bubbles formed and popped at the side of his mouth, and Greasy said, 'Oh God . . . '

Drift staggered backward two steps, his body sagging as he moved, then he dropped to his knees and fell over onto his back. Greasy stood still, hunched against the door, his breath coming in shivered bursts. Drift offered up small gurglings and whimperings and then these stopped.

I've just killed a man, thought Greasy. And what's more it was one of the few people who treated me decent. He crept over to the old man but he appeared to have breathed his last. He heard a motion off to his left, in the dark. Someone was there. He crouched low and edged toward the door, saying 'Who's there? I know you're over there. You saw it all. I was defending myself.' Then he heard a low nicker and a horse's face appeared in a shaft of light. Greasy sighed out loud, the relief loosening his chest. But what was he going to do now?

I have to make this look like an accident, he thought, or better yet like that stranger did it. But what if I'm wrong and Mrs Winters is still in the house? What then? He stood there, not looking down at Drift. His shivering lessened. The thought of that woman and a warm house and warm food and those tight dresses might take a bit of investigating before he decided on a course of action.

Outside the snow accumulated on the bare ground, nothing but a light dusting, but it was going to keep on, he knew. Better to hole up here. No, Winters would be home and he'd probably assume the worst and kill Greasy. The man had a temper on him, he'd seen it all those years ago during the range war, and Greasy had no idea just what Winters would do once he found out Greasy had killed the man who, everyone knew, had been like a father to Winters.

He left his horse by the barn and made his way across the yard to the end of the house. There was still no warm, welcoming glow of an oil lantern from inside, no smoke from the chimney, and the door was still open. He startled a white chicken and kicked at it as it squawked away from him.

Once again he found himself peeking in through an opened door. 'Hello?' he said, quiet this time, not quite poking his head in all the way, knowing what happened the last time. He waited, listening for any sound that might give away a person hiding. But he heard nothing and decided that since the light was fading he should get on with it or get out. The house was as neat as he expected it to be. He could tell a woman kept the place. There were curtains in the two windows and a table cloth on the dining table, a jar with some sort of late season greens stuck in the middle of it all. Why women thought they needed weeds to look at when you ate was beyond him. Some things, he figured, you'd just never get to the bottom of. One of 'em was women.

There was a loaf of bread under a towel on the countertop by the dry sink. He bit hunks off while he walked through the little home. He found the Winters' bedroom and jumped straight onto the bed, flopping and rolling there for a minute on the thick quilts. He got up, though, when he remembered his knack for falling asleep when he had a little whiskey in him. Wouldn't do for Winters to come home and find him sound asleep on the bed, with Uncle

Drift dead in the barn and the man's wife missing.

For that matter, he thought, it wouldn't do to have him come driving on up with that mule and find Greasy standing in his house and eating his bread, let alone sleeping. He swallowed down a few more hunks of bread, rubbed his chapped hands together, and in minutes he had the place turned upside down.

The only item of value he found that was small enough to take with him was an old gold pocket watch with a flip-open case. He stuffed it into a pant's pocket. Sell that somewhere down the road. He went back through to the kitchen and now he could barely see. The light was leaving fast. He went through the few cupboards and then his eyes rested on a corner shelf and a smile spread across his face. A whiskey bottle, nearly full, sat up there just waiting for him. He grabbed it with a giggle and took a quick pull before recorking it and thrusting it behind his belt. Good quality liquor. Should have known, he thought.

He looked around for matches, found them by the stove in a wall-mounted holder, and lit the lantern on the kitchen counter. He tossed the match on the floor and noticed it was still burning. He went to stomp it out and stayed his foot. Maybe a fire wasn't such a bad idea. Better and more complete if he lit it up inside and out. The house and the barn, too. It would do two things at once — get rid of any evidence that he was ever there and Drift would be taken care of at the same time. And as a bonus it would bring Winters down a notch or two. He grinned as he struck a match.

The tablecloth flared up fast. He realized too late that he should have started in the bedroom. Now his way was blocked by a mass of smoke. Too much to bother battling through. The place would be gone in no time, so it didn't really matter. He went outside with the lantern, a handful of matches, the whiskey, and the loaf of bread. The wind blew out the lantern within seconds and he had a devil of a time getting the match flames to catch on anything around the edge of the house. It grabbed in a few places and he sheltered the tiny flames until they seemed like they would make it on their own.

As he made his way back around the house, into the driving wind and snow, he cursed himself out loud for not grabbing some clothes, a quilt from the bed, anything that might help to keep him warm. He looked in the door. There was more thick smoke than flame, though he could see the flicker of orange tongues now and again in the middle of the roiling smoke. Oh well, at least he had the whiskey. Better than a hundred blankets.

He took another bite of bread and headed back to the barn, one hand holding his hat down tight against his head. Lighting the barn from the outside proved to be the same difficult process as it had been with the house. He gave up and stood still, listening. He heard nothing but the waxing and waning of the wind, felt big, wet snowflakes dabbing his face. He wanted a fresh horse and thought he might as well grab a saddle while he was at it. But the thought of going back in there with Drift in the middle of the barn floor bothered him. He looked over at his horse. It was skinny, and looked shriveled and shrunken compared to the horse he knew was in that stall in there. He made up his mind and went inside.

It was the same as before, only darker. He'd left the lantern by the house, tossed it in a clump of old grasses, but now wished he kept it. The little tack room had plenty of saddles, saddle blankets, bridles, everything he could want. He went to the stall first and there in the near dark was a large black horse. He couldn't be sure but he thought it might be Drift's. If so, it was a big, majestic beast. He spoke to it, held out a hand, and the horse reared up, his front legs a whirr of hoofs and gleaming black hair. Greasy got out of the stall just in time. His own nag looked better with every passing minute.

A new saddle, though, would be most welcome. He fumbled in the dark in the tack room, flicking one match after another into service. Finally he reached his last match. He could not find the rest of the tack he needed and just threw the saddle to the floor. He settled for a small sack of corn, tossed the match to the floor where it ignited straw, didn't seem capable of continuing the job, and just smoked and sputtered.

He glanced back toward where the road emerged from the trees, saw no one, and mounted his horse. He thought of the stranger. He'd been generous and he had promised that there was more money to be had. Well, might not have been a promise, more like a hint. But a hint was enough. He pretty much knew where that man was headed. With any luck he could catch up with him at his camp this very night. He was a safer bet than those gyps anyway. The more he thought about them, the less convinced he was that they would be worth the effort. If they had gold, why didn't they have shoes? Probably something to do with being a gyp. Besides, odds of running into Winters were pretty good if he headed back out the ranch lane to the main road. No, he'd stick with the one he'd seen with money, even if it meant heading into the woods. He still had daylight left. Might as well make the most of it.

The wind and snow whistled right up his shirt. The snow increased, covering everything with a thickening layer of white. He pulled his coat collar up high, yanked his hat down low, and poked the horse in the belly, directing it between the house and barn, out the old logging road, and toward the mountains. He looked back once and saw bits of flickering flame at one end of the house and at the barn, by the big open door. He smiled for just a second, then with one hand on the neck of the whiskey bottle he turned back toward the mountains.

6

'Ol' Lip, if this storm wasn't coming I wouldn't bother checkin' on these beasts today, but I haven't seen them in more than a month. As it is I'll have to come back out on horseback to check them again if the snow amounts to anything at all.'

Niall often talked out loud to Lip or whatever beast he happened to be with. Lippy was the only one to indicate he'd heard him, usually with a distinctive twitch of his ears. It never failed to amaze Niall.

He reined Lippy in at the point where a rough forest trail barely wide enough for his wagon broke in a southerly direction from the main road. It would take him through a plateau forest before opening out into his lower pastureland. It was easier to reach from home but he figured he had enough light left in the day to swing down, check on the remaining stock, and head home on the roundabout road he and Drift cut in a few years back. He guessed the stock were fine, though he knew he couldn't do much if he found any in trouble, or worse, missing. But with this storm coming in, he could not pass by a few miles to the north and not make the attempt to check on them. They were his livelihood, after all. The seed stock for next year's herd. He was justifying the detour, he knew, because Jenna and Drift both would tell him to leave well enough alone until after the storm had passed.

He looked to the south where the land fell away gradually into a rolling forest of spruce and cedar. And it was all his, part of the original plot they fought so hard for eight years ago. Winter's War, as it was still called around these parts, was a long time ago, but every so often, such as now, the memories were fresh enough that anger filled him again. It didn't help that Bert

Dibbs brought it up every darn time he went into town. He genuinely liked old Bert but if he was going to keep that up, one of these days Niall knew he was going to lose his temper and let him have a heaping helping of a piece of his mind. He smiled and shook his head. If he had to guess he'd say Esther already tore into Bert pretty good over it.

He pinched the collar of his coat tighter around his neck against the increasing wind that dogged him from town. I have to make sure I get back at least by dark tonight, otherwise Jenna's going to think I'm slipping back into my old ways of getting home later and later, not meaning to but getting caught up in my work so much so that I lose track of time. He understood her concern, but he couldn't stand the thought of not giving the place his all.

He remembered that night a few weeks back when he finally got home, bone-tired and well after dark. He'd left Uncle Drift to take care of the place, he was getting too old to spend long days on the trail or in the woods. By the time Niall dragged in it was late and Jenna had been waiting for him, as usual, bringing out the hot food off the back of the stove where she'd kept it warming.

It tasted good and he told her so, but when she finally did speak it was to tell him that he wouldn't know good food from bad because he was never home when he said he was going to be and by the time he finally stumbled in it was overcooked and not what she meant it to be. She'd stood then, and turned away from him.

He told her it was fine, just fine, and tried to hug her from behind, but that night she'd had all she was going to take from him. 'What about the life you're missing out on while always looking toward the future?' she'd asked. 'Live for now, Niall, not for a future that might never come. Look what we've been through. I didn't put up with that so I'd never see you.' He understood what she was saying, but he said that this was the only way he knew how to live. 'If I don't plan for our future, it never will come to be.'

She teared up, tossed her hands in the air, and walked right out the front door, no shawl, no nothing to keep her warm. It was late summer by that time and getting nippy at night in the hills. He'd gone after her, saying her name, and she said, 'Please leave me alone.' And she'd never spoken to him before like that, not in nearly eight years of marriage.

Uncle Drift had sauntered over from the barn for his usual night-time cup of coffee with them, and said, 'What'd you do, boy?'

Niall smiled at the memory as he guided Lippy through the ruts in the logging road he'd cleared over the past few months. Just like Drift to assume Niall was at fault, especially where Jenna was concerned. They discussed it and Drift had agreed with her on this count. It appeared they both thought Niall spent too much time working and too little time about the place. 'So your biggest complaint is that I work too hard?' he said to Drift. 'I'm just making sure our future is secure, especially out here where so much in life is uncertain.'

'Now, boy,' Drift said, 'before you fly off the handle and think the whole world's against you, just think on what we're saying.' And of course they were right. He'd spent the last couple of years largely in a clouded, driven haze.

She was gone for hours that night and it scared him. He determined then and there to change his ways. He took the next morning off and drove Jenna to town as a surprise. And in a stolen moment he cornered Esther at the store and ordered the spinning wheel he'd been thinking of ordering for a long time, but somehow never finding the time. She told him it might take as little as a month, but certainly no longer than three months to get there. Too late for their anniversary, which was coming up quick, but Esther thought maybe by

Christmas. Better late than never, he told himself.

In the meantime, he worked hard to turn things around, leaving off a task earlier than he was accustomed, loading the wagon before the sun went down. It hadn't been easy, but he'd tried. And judging from Jenna's happy face he was successful. And she was right, the food tasted better. He even teased her about it.

'And now here I am, Lip, lookin' like I'm going to be late again.'

He looked up at the sky as if it might tell him a bit more about the coming storm, and said, 'We'll give it a quick look-see, as Uncle Drift would say. Then we'll head right on home, maybe even get there in time for supper.'

He had to work Lippy harder than usual, and he knew the animal didn't want to leave the relative comfort of the primary road. 'I know how you feel, old fella, but it won't take long.' In addition to the cattle, he'd thought of the stand of Douglas fir. He'd kept half an eye on them for years. If he could thin them out, he'd be doing the rest of the trees a favor, and he figured he could make some sorely needed money at the same time. Getting the logs to market would be the trick. But the cattle rep in Hinckley mentioned rumblings that timber speculators were eyeing this region for likely sources of lumber for the building boom going on all over the north-west.

Niall wondered if he could beat them to it, clear some of his land in the process, and make money on the timber at the same time. All of this was a long way off, if at all, but it would be worth paying attention now to the trees, eyeing them as a speculator might. His land bordered the Shoshone River at the southern edge. He pondered on the feasibility of floating the logs to market.

This would be the only day until spring he'd be able to sneak off there for a look-see. Give him something to ruminate over during the long winter months when they would be pretty much holed up at the ranch. He estimated it would only take him a couple of hours out of his way, though he had never gotten to it from this side. In the past they'd always gone in from the north-east.

The wagon was narrow and Lippy was good on rough terrain. The trees were sparse enough that going forward should pose little problem. But, as they wheeled off the road and into the level but rutted trail, Niall, not used to second-guessing himself, had to clamp a hand onto his hat as a vicious gust of icy air swooped low over the trees and slammed them broadside. Lippy brayed and shook his head and Niall leaned into it, clutching the reins with one hand and squeezing shut his eyes momentarily.

The gust died quickly and he said, 'No, sir. I'll be damned if I'm going to be bullied into changing my mind because of a skittish mule and a little bit of wind.' He snapped the reins once and headed into the woods.

It was a small holding, but it was all theirs. There was no lending institution involved. The barn was piled with the two cuttings of sweetgrass and he and Uncle Drift had finished the door two days ago, none too soon for the cold, but hopefully in plenty of time for snow. They'd each taken turns at the forge to fashion the crude pin hinges, but they were serviceable and should last for a good, long time. And that was how he approached everything about the place. So that it would last. And what's more so that they would outlast him. He knew the only reason a man does something to that extreme is to ensure a legacy for his descendents. And that only could happen with the assurance that children would be forthcoming. So far she'd not told him that there was any such possibility for them. Nor had she indicated that it wasn't to be. So he hoped and overbuilt for the future.

Too late, Niall felt the wagon slump. He pitched forward, lifting him from his seat. With his hands outstretched, he caught himself on Lippy's rump and balanced there, assessing the situation. It was not good.

'What the hell happened, Lip?' Niall said as he pushed himself off Lippy's rump and looked down at the mess at his feet. Lip was knee deep in a marsh and looking around himself, his ears back, as if to say, 'Now who put this swamp here?'

The front wheels of the wagon were sunk to the axle, the same depth as Lippy's mostly covered knees. The mule just stood there seeming embarrassed. Niall pushed off and worked his way to the back of the wagon. The rear wheels were on dry ground. They'd wandered into a low, marshy patch. He should have known, given the amount of water-loving scrub cedars around. But he hadn't noticed them, drifting into reverie as he was. He cursed himself for not paying attention. Lippy lowered his head, his ears back. He was trying to lift his feet but the wagon had slumped far enough forward that it forced the traces against him and prevented him from moving. Every time he tried, the wagon snugged tight behind him.

'Not your fault, old-timer. All mine this time. I should have been paying attention.'

He hopped down, unbuttoned his coat, and started unloading the packed wagon. In the snow, anything with wheels was a mess of trouble and near impossible to move. Especially with the amounts of snow they were in for each year. Hard enough to pick your way through on horseback, let alone pulling a wagon when the roadway's packed in with eight, ten, or more feet. One year they got twelve feet in the passes.

As he pitched sack after sack of flour and corn meal and beans and oats, stacking them on crates off to the side of the crude trail, he heard the wind slicing through the treetops above them, swaying every tree around him.

And to think he'd almost made it. If he hadn't decided to turn off for a look at the cedar stand and the stock, neither of which required his urgent attention, he would almost be home by now.

Thankfully they were far enough in the woods that they were fairly protected by the wind. As he worked his stomach growled. It had been hours since he'd had anything more than a handrolled and a few swigs of cold water from the canteen. He could almost taste his wife's thick venison stew with dumplings bubbling on top, moist enough to be gummy, and just the way he liked them. She mentioned before he left that she might make that, have it waiting for him when he got back today. He hoped so.

'Curse me for a fool, Lippy,' he said, and then he looked up from his work and noticed the big animal's withers shivering. He worked faster, shouting words of encouragement to the mule. Niall knew that the near-frozen swamp muck, without benefit of being able to move his legs, must be freezing Lippy's hoofs and joints. When at last he had slid out the crate containing Jenna's spinning wheel, the last item in the wagon, he barely paused before blocking the rear wheels with an old, half-rotted log and then unhooking the traces.

The darkening woods yielded all manner of sticks, deadfalls, and bark — anything he could gather to get him out on his belly toward the front of the mule. It wouldn't do for him to get bogged down as well, or too wet too early in the going. This was almost like retrieving someone from a frozen pond. Only now, luckily, there was a bottom not too far down.

Lippy quivered all over. 'I'm working as fast as I can, Lip. Hang in there.' Niall rubbed the old mule's jaw. He grasped the reins and pulled them toward him to encourage the mule. Nothing. He pulled hard on the reins and Lippy jerked his head away from him as if to say, 'Go on without me. I'm finished.'

'You ain't giving up just yet, old boy. We have too much work to do on this spread of ours.' He crawled backward, holding onto the reins. Lippy only had to make it though five or six feet of muck, and it probably got shallower the closer he got to Niall's edge. But convincing a mule to do something he had his mind dead set against doing, Niall found long ago, was like convincing Uncle Drift that he'd be better off not heading to the poker tables after he visited the bar for a few hours. And yet every month it was the same old story. He'd come riding back home hunched over in his saddle, sore headed and light in the coin purse.

'Now Jenna,' he'd say, even before she said anything. And most of the time she never did. The look on their faces was enough to keep Niall smiling for hours.

'Lip,' said Niall, pulling off his coat and rolling up his shirt sleeves. 'We're going to try something different.' The light had definitely shifted in the past twenty minutes they'd been here in the swamp. He crawled back out there on his belly, and inhaling deeply he slid the back of his hand against Lippy's foreleg and reached down into the frigid, stiffening muck.

'God, Lippy. I had no idea it was this cold.' Still he worked to pull away the thick, black goo from in front of each of the mule's forelegs. As he slid back to the shore, massaging his numb arms, Lippy lurched forward. He's trying, thought Niall. By God, he's trying. He scrambled to the dry ground behind him and grabbed a long, stiff branch.

'I'm sorry, Lippy, but I have to do it.' And he snapped the old mule hard on the rump. That seemed to make all the difference. Rarely if ever had he been subjected to the buggy whip, and so Lippy lurched forward and thrashed his way closer and closer to the near shore. He slowly gained higher ground and Niall watched the muck-covered legs rise with each lunge toward the shore.

He continued whipping the beast in encouragement, knowing that a mule that gives up, as with a horse or a cow, will give up completely and just die right there in its tracks. It's as if someone scoops out all their will power. And it was still one of the most frustrating things to Niall, never getting any easier, no matter how many years he'd spent in the company of beasts of burden.

When Lippy emerged fully from the deceiving little patch of marsh, he trembled all over. Niall stripped live cedar branches of their green foliage and rubbed Lippy to encourage his circulation, especially in those legs. When he felt that he could do no more he led the mule to the rear of the leaning wagon and rigged up rope to each side of the axle underneath, then mostly with words of encouragement, Lippy twitched that wagon up and out of the little marsh.

Niall had Lippy work the wagon back enough so that when he rerigged the mule they worked the wagon to the uphill side of the marsh, threading through the trees, until they could regain the trail.

There was no time now to check on the stock, something he may have been able to do had he not bothered to take this detour off his larger, intended stock route. He would just have to make as good a time as they could on the crude road to home. It meant another three hours of traveling in close woods without proper gear for a night out. Let alone the fact that Uncle Drift would head out looking for him.

Niall loaded the wagon as quickly as he could, taking care to wedge everything in well, and then lashed it all down again with ropes, should they encounter any more surprises. The last thing he did before heading out was to water Lippy and hand feed him a few handfuls of corn.

'Get along, Lip,' he finally said, sitting in the wagon seat once again. He cleaned his arms off as best he could with dried leaves and cedar greens but the marsh muck threw a pungent smell, one that reached him even through his coat and gloves. He was thankful, though, that matters hadn't ended up far worse. He knew they would have to make good time now as they would both be getting cold. Best to keep Lip moving. A snowstorm was no place for wet and cold creatures, he thought, cursing himself for the wasted time and the near-tragic outcome.

7

The old woman spoke to her husband in rare English: 'The storm is much worse now.' He stared straight ahead, but the snow accumulated on his eyelashes and soon he had to blink hard to melt it. She knew he would not dare wipe his face with his hand, though his eyelashes and moustaches were now covered with snow.

Several minutes passed. 'The man Winters offered us a place to stay during the storm.' She watched her husband's face; it could be so like stone sometimes. 'Just for the storm.'

He closed his eyes. When he opened them he was looking at her. He pulled back on the reins and the black pony, whose top half was now mostly white but for a strip of melted snow along her back, came to a stop.

'Is this what you want? To stop in a

stranger's house as beggars?'

She opened her mouth to protest and he cut her off, saying, 'Good. That is what we do.' And he maneuvered the little pony around until they swayed back toward the side road.

But for her, she could tell, he would stay out alone, battling the storm until he was frozen through. But she also knew that, as always, he would do anything for her. As long as it was her idea each time. As long as he could appear angry at the very thought of altering course. If it got them to shelter and warmth, she could live with that.

After a few minutes she passed an arm through his and squeezed his sleeve. He did not change expression, still staring ahead, but he leaned into her and she rested her head against his shoulder and smiled. He would never change and she guessed that neither would she.

After a few miles she sat upright again and kept her gaze on the side of the road. In this snow the lane to the man Winters' home would be easy to miss. Scarcely ten minutes later they rolled to a stop in the road at the entrance to the lane. He turned to her once, sighed a deep, chesty sigh, and clicked and clucked the pony into the lane. Within minutes they were riding under a canopy of evergreens. The snow was much lighter and the wind, though they could hear it far above, barely reached them.

'Oh, this is beautiful,' she said, holding a hand up and touching the lowest hanging branches.

He nodded and smiled. 'It is not unlike the old country. Oh, the forests there. You remember? I hunted all through them in my youth. I knew them like my own hands.' He smiled, his bushy eyebrows rising to meet like caterpillars dancing. It was good to see him smile. It had been too long since he had smiled. He looked down at his hands, turning them over as if ashamed to look, and all too soon the smile faded. He settled forward, his elbows resting on his knees.

'There is nothing for me to do but go from here to there, here to there. I have nothing more to take pride in.' He held up a hand and looked at her. 'I was a craftsman. I could work all day. I know many things. I can build fine furniture and I can tend the biggest flock of sheep. You couldn't see how far such a flock could stretch.' He faced the lane ahead and said, 'Pah!'

She squeezed his arm and said nothing. Up ahead the trees gave way to open space. And in minutes they had reached the mouth of the lane. From there it opened into a meadow, the wagon track continuing over a rise and ending, she assumed, at the house and barn she saw in the distance. 'Friendly,' she said in Basque, half in warning to him, gripping his arm. Let him take it to mean what he will, she thought. She was relieved that they would have a bit of relief from traveling, if only for a night.

Well before they reached the yard they saw that something was wrong. Gray-black smoke rolled from the house, but not from the chimney. He snapped the reins and they trotted up to a water trough between the house and barn. He saw no buckets and retrieved theirs from its hook underneath the wagon.

'Yell for help!' he told his wife as she climbed down from the wagon. Their dog, Bella, barked inside the caravan. He dipped the bucket and ran to the house. The snow kept this fire from spreading, but as he circled the outside of the house, dousing the random patches of flame, he kicked a scorched oil lantern. So, maybe this was no accidental fire.

When he was satisfied that the outside fires were doused he dipped his bucket again in the trough and ran up the steps and into the house. The smoke was thick but he saw little fire. A section of the roof was damaged above

102

what looked like the far end of the kitchen, judging from the remains of a dining table. One bucket of water was all it took to convince him that the coals would not flare up again. Again he suspected the wet snow of the storm kept the house from burning.

'Hello! Hello!' he shouted, but received no answer. He pulled the top of his shirt over his mouth and nose and held it there with a hand as he ventured beyond the large central stone chimney. Two other rooms, but they were empty of people. The smoke was less thick in these two rooms. There was a small, two-pane window but he could not figure out how to open it, if it opened at all. He looked again at the large bed, the chest, and chair, the comfortable furnishings of a home, though everything looked jumbled and out of place. He grunted and left. The barn would need attending to as well.

He heard his wife's screams before he reached the porch steps. He descended them in two bounds and ran through the snow, past their wagon with Bella still barking inside, and met his wife as she ran to him from the direction of the barn. 'There is a man . . . ' she was trying to catch her breath, gulping air, and covering her mouth with her hand. 'A man is . . . '

'What?' he said, holding her arms. 'Did he hurt you?'

She shook her head violently. 'He is dead!'

He looked at her a moment, then said, 'Go to the wagon. Go now. You will be safe there.'

He gripped the handle of the bucket and walked toward the half-open barn door. He turned once, saw his wife still staring at him, and motioned for her to go back toward the wagon. She stood still, her hands covering her mouth.

He pushed open the barn door and there was the man, on his back in the middle of the barn with a hay fork standing upright from his chest. The little man stood there panting. He had fought in four wars with many battles in them, had seen countless dead men, and it never became easier to see such things. Whoever set the house alight must also have done this horrible thing. And he could still be here. He pulled back from the door, his eyes wide, scanning everything inside as he did so, then turned and hurried back to his wife. 'We must go.'

'Yes, we should go back to town. To find — '

'No!'

'Then we should wait for him here?'

'No! Do you not understand? They will think we did this. This house fire' — he waved his soot covered arm at the smoking house behind him — 'the dead man . . . all of this.'

She stared at him as though he were a stranger.

How could he make her understand? 'Have you forgotten that to them we are 'gyps,' nothing more? You heard how they spoke of us back there. They hate the very sight of us. It is the same everywhere.'

'But the man was nice. The one who owns this ranch. He was kind to us. He will need help.'

'Pah . . . they are all the same.'

'Now you sound like them,' she said, turning from him.

He handed her the bucket and ran back to the house. A minute later he returned, his face stony and serious. He thrust a blanket, a dead turkey, still feathered, and a handful of vegetables into her arms.

She stared and tried to push the items back at him. 'This is stealing,' she hissed.

'No. This is payment for saving his house. For not letting it burn.' But she could see on his face that he did not believe himself. He helped her up to the seat. 'Where will we go? Back to the road?' she said.

'No, we cannot. We would meet him and he would not understand.' He looked ahead, toward the mountains. 'We will still head east, but that way.' He nodded ahead at the snowed path between the house and barn that stretched east toward the peaks. 'We must head into the mountains.'

'No, no, no,' she said, shaking her head.

'We are mountain people. We will find a way through.'

'We are *from* mountain people. But that does not mean we *are* mountain people. My love,' she turned to him, a desperate look in her eyes, 'the difference could kill us out there.'

He ignored her comment and said, 'There is more shelter in the mountains.' And with a last look behind them, he snapped the reins on the little pony's back. His wife touched the patchwork quilt in her lap and shook her head.

8

It was the bone-numbing cold that pulled him from sleep. Niall opened his eyes and for the briefest moment he could see nothing but the redness of blood all around him. He yelled, 'No!', scaring himself into full wakefulness. Lippy jerked his head up, his nose was nearly resting on the ground. Niall's breath came in gasps and his chest worked as if he had just been chased for miles.

It had been a bad dream, nothing more. He gritted his teeth in anger at having fallen asleep. It was unthinkable. He must have been more tired than he thought to allow this to happen. And Lippy, too. He had never known the old mule to stop on the trail. Lip always had an unerring sense of direction and rarely slowed to less than a walk, especially when they were headed for home.

As he regained control of his breathing, Niall blinked hard, opened and closed his eyes a number of times and forced himself to look at everything surrounding him. The wind's intensity increased, and the snow fell thicker than ever. Lippy's back and head wore an inch of heavy, wet snow, as did the wagon and its contents, and Niall himself was covered with it. He stretched his arms, pulled off his hat, and slapped it against his leg, then shook the reins still looped in his left hand. He looked behind and their tracks to this point were covered.

He was still on the trail, though the sun was nearly gone. Judging from the shadows of the trees on the snow, it would not be long before the day's light dropped completely, and with it the temperature. He swished the reins back and forth and said, 'Got to get home now, Lippy.' He clicked his tongue and snapped the reins on the mule's back. Lippy started forward at a slow, stiff pace, clumps of snow sliding from his now moving body. And within minutes of urging they were once again heading home.

Niall felt guilty for driving the mule harder than he normally would have but the weather was worsening. And as he leaned forward, taking in huge draughts of icy air, he knew that the real reason he was hurrying had more to do with the feeling of dread that filled him. And it was all because of that dream. He couldn't recall the specifics, but the feelings of gloom and foreboding were so vivid, so real. 'Heyah!' he shouted and cracked the reins on Lippy's back. The little wagon bounced and clunked through the rutted logging trail, and Lippy did his best to maintain a brisk pace at Niall's urging, despite the difficult terrain. Not for the last time that day did Niall curse himself for choosing this slow-going route. 'I'd be home by now . . . ' He let the oath whip from his mouth in the cold wind.

9

The last of the day's light leaked away, though it was not until much later that the stranger finally stopped. The wind grew throughout the afternoon, stirring the snow into a white wall, at times impossible to see through. He dismounted and led his horse just off the rough trail they followed and into a small clearing in the evergreens. Under the deepening snow, brown wisps of rangy grasses rustled and snapped under their feet. Moving as if he had been there before, he tied off his horse to the stub of a low, dead branch. Then he appeared by Jenna's side, untying her wrists from the pommel, though he left them bound together.

All afternoon she thought of ways to hurt him. She might land enough of a kick to daze him, maybe even knock him senseless. That's a joke, she thought. I'm so cold I can't even keep my head upright. Before she knew what was happening, he pulled her from her horse. She landed on her side in the snow. He grabbed the rope binding her wrists together and lifted her to her feet. He dragged her and she tried to keep up with him, stumbling, only able to say, 'Stop it! I can walk!' But he acted as if he hadn't heard her as he pulled her to the base of a wide, old pine.

'Here,' he said, and tossed a wool blanket on her lap. She manipulated her tied hands enough to drape the blanket about her shoulders, and pulled it over her head, squeezing it closed in front of her, keeping her hands inside.

She watched him through a gap in the blanket as he built a small fire, too small for cooking. He huddled over it, warming his hands. In a few minutes he stripped the horses' gear and watered them at a nearby stream. Then he tied them off and fed them.

He pulled jerky and hard biscuits

from a sack and tossed a bit of both at her feet. In defiance, she ignored the food for a few minutes, but it didn't seem to matter to him. She grabbed the food and ate it too fast. It just left her hungry for more. He drank from a canteen, then plugged it and dropped it at her feet. She wiped the mouth of the vessel, then drank as he resumed his spot across from her, hunched over the fire, warming his hands.

'What do you want from us? Why are you doing this?'

He didn't even look at her. It was as if he didn't hear her, as if he were alone.

After ten minutes, despite the blanket, she was still so cold she couldn't keep her teeth from rattling together. She pushed herself to her knees and crawled forward the ten feet to the skimpy fire, keeping her eyes on him the entire time. Again, no response. She sat across from the fire, just within his reach, but she kept to herself, huddled only as close as she dared. After a minute like this he seemed to melt backward to the edge of the dark, beyond the scant light cast by the tiny blaze. But he was there, sitting cross-legged, also wrapped in a blanket, his hat pulled low. She leaned forward over the fire and warmed her hands.

The heat was welcome. Before too long it emboldened her thoughts. She gazed down into the now-glowing embers, orange like a strong sunset. What could she do with her hands bound? Kick the hot coals at him. That would only make him angry and ruin her source of heat.

Her gaze fell on the small pile of snapped branches he gathered to feed the fire. Some of the ends were sharp where he broke them to length. If she could secret one under her skirts, slide it inside her boot, she might use it at some opportune moment to stab him. She inched her way toward the stack, leaning as far as she dared without shifting her knees. If he were near sleep she might get away with it. She leaned a bit further, her fingertips almost touching a stout, knife-length section of branch, the ends both jagged.

He stood in one motion from his seated position, the blanket falling from his shoulders. He had seen her. Somehow he sensed what she was up to. She sat upright and tucked her hands back under her blanket, holding it tight and looking down. With two steps he was behind her. She crouched low, tight with fear, not knowing what he was about to do.

A hand grabbed at the blanket and back of her dress collar, caught some of her hair with it. She uttered a quick shout as he dragged her back to the tree. He knelt before her, his hat still pulled low, and leaned over her. She pulled her legs up, her knees a sort of defense. He paused, pushed the blanket away from her feet, and pulled from his coat pocket a length of the same rough hemp he used on her wrists. He pulled her feet out so her legs straightened, then he tied her feet together. Even in her fear, she was thankful she wore boots, otherwise the rope would do the same as the wrist rope and chafe her ankles raw.

He pulled out his machete and she held her breath, afraid to close her eyes, too frightened to make a sound. He slipped it under the rope and sliced off the excess. Then he looped it low around her waist and tied it tight behind the tree.

He resumed his spot at the fire, sitting cross-legged, facing her with his hat pulled low. She didn't know what to make of him. Was he going to kill her? Was he really taking her back there to that evil place from so long ago? None of this made sense. She was so tired that despite her fear of him, of what he might do to her in the night, sleep clawed at her. Finally, she let sleep overcome her. Jenna had a feeling that morning would come early with this stranger.

10

It was dark, had been for hours by the time Niall guided Lippy into the yard from the trail leading up and out of the woods that grew close by the southern end of the house. From this trail he couldn't see the place fully until he was almost in the yard. But when they pulled up he knew, even in the dark, that something was very wrong. There were no lights in the house, none coming from the barn or beyond, from Uncle Drift's quarters.

A reversing gust of wind smacked him full in the face and the smell of smoke enveloped him. It was not usual woodstove smoke. It was pungent and cloying, like moldy grain.

The wind was undecided tonight, slamming first from the north, then the east, only to regroup itself and buffet them from the south a moment later.

No wonder he hadn't smelled the smoke until he was in the yard. He had expected a candle burning in the kitchen window. He raised a gloved hand above his eyes. He squinted against the driving snow and drew Lippy up to the house. All of a sudden the situation became clear to him. He leapt from the wagon, his boot heel catching on the edge and sending him to his knees.

'Jenna!' He yelled her name over and over, even as he rose to his feet running, clunking up the steps to the house. His throat burned from the smoke. He yanked the door open and felt his way into the room. The fire was out, no flames or sparks anywhere. But he smelled the pervasive stench from a smoldering fire. 'Jenna!' he yelled, the stink of old smoke choking his voice, forcing dry coughs from him. He staggered about the room, colliding with what was left of their table and chairs. The cold wind buffeted him from above and he realized that part of the roof was missing. How much he couldn't tell, nor did he care. He felt his way into the other two rooms, shouting his wife's name the entire time.

He made his way back outside and ran past Lippy, who had walked forward and was drinking at the trough. Niall made it to the barn and against the white snow he saw the glow of coals in midair. He ran toward it yelling, 'Uncle Drift! Drift!' As he got close, he saw that the coals were the nearly dead embers of the tag-end of boards burned from the bottom up. He pushed snow against them with his boot and they sizzled and steamed out.

This, he knew, was no accident. A house might burn, a barn might burn, and yes, the wind might also carry sparks from one to the other, but it was unlikely, especially on a night such as this and at such a distance. And from the looks of things, the fire sprouted from the base of a building, just the spot where a man might start a fire, hoping to nurture it into flame. He thought of the hay inside and ran to the big double doors, closed over but not latched. He yanked open the outermost door, the snow not thick enough to stop it swinging. Inside the familiar smells of the barn met his nostrils, mixed with the faint stink of smoke.

'Uncle Drift! Jenna!' There was no answer.

He groped his way to the tack room, just inside to the right, and found the lantern they used for early and late chores high up on its peg. They had its mate in the house to travel back and forth in the dark. He tore off his sodden gloves, pulling at the fingertips with his teeth, and with trembling hands he pulled matches from his shirt breast pocket, his tobacco pouch falling to the floor.

'Come on, come on,' he urged himself in a hoarse whisper, then shouted, 'Uncle Drift? Jenna?'

He dragged a match against his pants leg three, four, five times, snapping it, finally, in half. He grabbed another, nearly screaming now his inner rage was so great. And he flicked it with his numb thumbnail. It flamed and he raised the mantle of the lantern and lit the wick. He carried the lantern into the main barn and walked to the center of the open space, holding it up high and turning to take in the quiet space.

All appeared to be in order. Drift's horse, Mackie, was in his stall. Was Jenna's Sweet Baby in hers, too? And what of his own horse, Slate? He walked closer, holding the lantern out in front of him. Mackie backed away into the dark stall and nickered. And then Niall stubbed his boots and something hard bounced off his arm. He jumped back a pace, the lantern swinging, and brought it around to see his Uncle Drift on his back on the hay-strewn floor, the hay fork sticking out of his chest, the handle standing nearly perfectly upright. Niall's breath left him and for a long moment he was capable only of staring down at his Uncle Drift in this horrifying pose.

He knelt and touched Drift's face. But it was cold. Despite his every hope to feel warmth, there was just cold, still skin. He moved the lantern next to Drift's shoulder and the old man's eyes stared up at him.

'I'm sorry, Uncle Drift.' Niall's voice shook, not yet of rage, not yet of the sadness that was to come, but of a strange mixture of the two. 'I don't know what happened, but I should have been here. I will never forgive myself for this and I will find who did this and I will make that bastard pay dearly.' His jaw ached from clenching it so tight and he shook all over with a rising anger that for the time being acted as a balm for his pain.

The possibilities of the situation hammered down on him all at once. If someone had done this to Uncle Drift, what of Jenna? Had she gone for help? Could it have been an accident? It was possible, surely. And yes, Jenna could have gone for help. He grabbed the lantern from the floor and crossed to the horse stall. Only Mackie remained. If Jenna had gone for help, where was his own horse, Slate? She would not have taken him, too. Jenna was afraid of the big gray gelding. Doubt once more crept in.

Somehow this occurred to them all — a day gone wrong. It happened to people. It happened to him today, a series of events that seems to get worse, each one surpassing the previous one until . . . But he was fooling himself. It was not the case here. The fires, the pitchfork in Drift's chest, these things spelled out the grim truth and reluctantly he accepted it. And again he cursed himself for taking the long way home that afternoon. For stopping at the mercantile longer than he should have. For leaving his wife and home and old uncle in the first place. They should all have gone. He clenched his fists until his fingers ached and the pain helped to clear his head.

He dragged Drift's saddle from the rail. Looking in the dim light for the rest of the rig, he knocked other gear to the floor, threw buckets and ropes out of his way, and finally dropped the saddle and shouted out loud in anger. He rubbed his eyes with a thumb and forefinger. Maybe this was another damned dream. He wished it was so, but he knew otherwise.

Jenna. He must concentrate on finding her. He would be no use to her if he rode out into the dark with no supplies, no plans. He would have to turn back if he were ill prepared. He opened his eyes and took a deep breath. Have to get organized. A few precious minutes now might make all the difference later.

Standing here regretting his decisions wasn't going to help find her. He forced himself to think. He had the lantern. Lippy would keep in the yard until he dealt with matters in here. He turned back to Uncle Drift and closed the old man's eyes. His hands were already clasped in front of his belly, as if he had prepared himself, as if he knew. Just like

Uncle Drift, he thought. He would know that a stiffened limb must be broken to be put at peace and he would have done this to help me.

Niall pulled on the fork and his uncle's chest lifted with it, then slipped from the tines. He tossed the fork against the wall and knew he would never use that tool again. Drift's boot heels left slight trails in the dirt as Niall dragged him into the tack room and laid him out there on the floor, draping a canvas tarp over him. He weighted the edges to help prevent critters from nosing around. He had no idea when he might return, or if he would return, or even where he was going, but at least Drift was in some presentable state of rest. It was all he could think of to do at the moment.

He looked down at the buckled length of canvas, at Uncle Drift, the man who had been, for most of Niall's life, closer to him than a father or brother. Not only had the man raised him but he had been his best friend as well. And now that he was in somewhat of a position to repay the old man but a fraction of the kindnesses and sacrifices he had made in his life on Niall's behalf, Drift was dead.

He still had, at his best guess, several hours of dark ahead of him and he didn't know where to go or what to do. He had to make sure Jenna wasn't here, hurt somewhere. The barn door caught in a gust of wind and slammed outward and he remembered Lippy, standing faithfully out there in the cold. The sooner he took care of Lip the sooner he could saddle up and go after Jenna. He would look here first, of course, but he sensed that she was long gone, and probably not because she wanted to.

But where had she gone? He was sure that Drift brought all the horses inside when the first signs of the storm presented themselves. So where was his big gray, Slate, and where was Jenna's bay, Sweet Baby? The only reasonable answer was that someone had taken them, either Jenna or someone else. But why not take Mackie, too? None of this made sense.

He dropped to his hands and knees and searched the floor for signs that might shed light on this situation. The floor was strewn with straw and scuffed dirt. A thought occurred to him and he returned to the tack room. Her saddle and gear were gone. The other two saddles remained, but Slate's bridle was gone. Was he being led? As a pack horse, maybe? Jenna wouldn't do that. If she were riding for help she would have saddled her own horse at best, not bothered with a second horse. Besides, he was a large gelding, and too unruly for her. Even Uncle Drift wasn't partial to him. Who would take him? Someone who knew horses. Slate was worth a pretty penny, but somehow he didn't think this had much to do with money.

He pushed out into the storm to retrieve Lippy, who was standing, head bowed with the wind, at the water trough. He swung the lantern in small, slow arcs, keeping a protective hand near the base where the wind might sneak under the glass globe. He kept close to the ground, hoping to see some sign of who might have been there, who might have done this thing. Every once in a while as the wind turned, a blast of smoke filled his lungs. He squinted through the snow, made it to the trough, and touched Lippy on the head. Lip wagged his oversize ears but kept his head down.

Niall left him there and went to the house. He looked down, hoping to find any sign in the snow, knowing that whatever happened would be covered well by the snow. If all this happened many hours before, as he suspected, then Jenna could have already ridden to town by the time he got there himself today. She didn't go that way. She was an experienced horsewoman. The odds of anything happening to her between here and there were slim. Especially in the decent weather that preceded this storm.

He made his way around the house

and down back to the root cellar but all seemed in order. He still couldn't see the roof but figured that whoever had torched it chose the wrong night of the year. The snow was heavy and wet enough that any possible sign was covered over. And it would only be worse by the morning.

He returned to the trough and bent to grab Lippy's reins looped on the snow below the mule's nose. As he bent, something caught his eye. Because of the general direction of the wind, there was a strip of bare mud, six inches wide, running the length of the trough. And there were prints squished into this mud. Human footprints. Bare feet. Just the toes and a bit of the foot behind them, but wide enough to be a man's and positioned as though he were standing close, possibly working the pump handle. Bare feet this time of year.

He'd only seen one person do such a thing and it wasn't Jenna, whose small feet would never leave such a print, nor would it be Uncle Drift, who would

129

never be caught dead barefoot any time of year. It was the little gypsy man. Had to be. It began to make sense and yet he didn't want to believe it. He hated to admit that Greasy was right.

Surely misfortune and bad deeds couldn't have followed those two older people. The man was nursing an anger of some sort, Niall was sure. He'd seen that pure cold look before. But to do this? He could scarcely believe it, yet it must be so. There was no other explanation. But why Jenna? Why would they take her? Unless they didn't take her. Just the horses. He pushed that thought from his mind as he hurried Lippy to the barn. He pulled the doors wide and led the mule and wagon inside.

Mackie nickered in the dark stall and Lippy answered with a tired noise from deep in his throat. Niall unhitched the old mule and led him to his stall, apologizing out loud to him for not being able to give him a decent rubdown tonight. But he had much to do. He hastily dumped a heaping bucket of feed corn into Lippy's trough and tossed in three great armloads of hay. Then he grabbed the lantern and headed back out the door, calling Jenna's name into the biting wind and snow. He spent much of an hour stumbling about the place, looking everywhere for his wife. Finally he admitted defeat and returned to the barn.

★ ★ ★

Niall loaded Mackie with Drift's saddle, the gear Mackie was accustomed to. He thought of what Greasy said earlier that day. Something about gypsies leaving nothing but bad luck behind. He jammed a sack full of jerked meat, half a loaf of bread, and apples, coffee, and his trail pot and cup, and packed it all in his saddle-bags. He bagged corn for the horse and retrieved Uncle Drift's Colt, along with his own, to make it a pair. He double-checked and jammed his Winchester in its leather scabbard and fastened two blankets to Mackie. He hoped the horse was up to the challenge of the steep trails and packed passes he knew that might lay ahead.

He rummaged in the house, among the overturned items of their bedroom, wondering now that it was someone looking to make money. If anything was missing he didn't see it, nor was he looking. He did find something that puzzled him greatly for a good few minutes, until he settled on a reasoned guess: he found a pair of brand new ash-and-hide snowshoes. Just his size. Then it occurred to him that they must be an anniversary gift for him from Jenna. He stood holding them in the wreckage of their bedroom. Would he and Jenna see their big day? And what would it mean this year?

He gathered all his ammunition and found his rabbit-fur hat. He peeled off his sheepskin jacket long enough to pull on two more layers of clothes, including another pair of socks and a sweater, both knitted by Jenna. Last he pulled on his sheepskin mittens.

He refused to let himself think of what might have happened to her, what could happen to her, though he spent plenty of time thinking of what the gypsies might want with her. He could only think that it might be a ransom of some sort. To those who obviously had little he might look like a wealthy man. That might mean they weren't far off.

The wind slowed to an insistent but steady blow from the north, and the snow still barreled down. He was nearly ready to go. It was still dark and he didn't care. The reflected light from the snow would have to serve him. He was more anxious to depart than he had ever been to begin anything in his life. The sooner he caught up with the gypsies, the sooner he could deal with them. They would not be difficult to find, even though their sign was covered in snow. But in which direction should he start? They must have headed east, but that would mean heading down the entrance road to the ranch. They wouldn't risk that, not knowing that he took an alternate route home. But what if they had? They might be well on their way toward Big Pine by now. He would catch them. A wagon like that could only travel so fast, and he was on horseback. He would find them.

★   ★   ★

The old driving trail ran down from the foothills against which the ranch nestled. The hills formed the base of Shiller's Peak and its attendant smaller mountains. At its height, the Peak was a daunting place of steep talus slopes and jagged outcroppings, traits shared by all the surrounding mountains. They only softened in appearance and hospitality when they lost their altitude and became foothills. And it was there, between the hills, that most of Niall Winters' usable land lay, though he also owned far up the slopes into the rugged reaches of Shiller's and other of the surrounding mountain-sides.

There had been enough to do for the past eight years since the range war, in establishing a herd, clearing stretches of good grazing land, and thinning the forests so that they, too, might be used as a source of income through the years. The logging, selectively and with an eye toward stewardship of the land, was something he felt an affinity for but had not, until they settled there, given the matter much thought. Logging the land had been Uncle Drift's idea.

More often than not he was right. And the old driving trail, used by early settlers decades before, cut right through a nearly impassable slice between Shiller's base and a smaller rocky knob, over foothills which were themselves more mountainous than anything seen back East, and on down through the spot they eventually chose for the ranch, before continuing on to merge with the road to town.

That town road became the more

preferred route for the infrequent traveler from East to this part of the country, since the driving trail was choked off in a substantial rock slide years before Niall and Drift settled there. Without travelers driving straight through their ranch, the trail now was rendered useless. Niall and Drift kept the lower portion of it somewhat passable and it proved useful for moving herds from one grazing ground to another. And Niall had an idea that when the time came it would prove equally useful for hauling timber. He planned on raising a team of oxen, now that his herd and grazing lands were well established.

Just beyond the yard the trees grew sparse but well and, as one traveled further from the ranch into the hills the forested sections thickened and waned at random near the trail. Nothing but a pure white, windswept lane punctuated with an increasing number of spruce and aspen, still black against the snow, stretched out into the shrouded hills beyond.

Before Niall led Mackie from the barn he looked down at Drift's body a last time. After a moment he spoke. 'Devil's in the details, like you always say, Uncle Drift.' He breathed deep. 'We're about to test that theory.' Mackie lowered his head, sniffed at his dead master's boots, and snorted. Niall pushed open the barn door. 'C'mon, Mackie.'

He spurred the black horse into the general center of the white lane and leaned low in the saddle, squinting down at the snow in what he knew was a futile attempt to find any sign of his wife's whereabouts. He criss-crossed the lane. He would go up the old trail for a few miles, he decided, and if he could find no reason to continue in that direction he would backtrack and take the ranch road, then head east toward Big Pine.

As he veered to the right side of the trail, Drift's pet phrase rang in his head, 'Devil's in the details,' and he wondered if he would ever know just what Drift meant by it. Details, details, Niall almost said the word aloud.

He neared the edge of the trail, lifting his head and blinking hard, melting the snow that collected on his eyelashes. As he opened his eyes something caught his eye on the nearest tree, a stout old white pine. He pulled Mackie closer. There on the trunk, trailside, level with his knee, Niall saw a fresh, raw scar in the bark, hacked into the trunk. This was not something he or Drift ever did. If they ever needed to mark a tree they did so a little easier than this. Neither of them would ever hack so savagely into a tree.

He looked behind him back toward the ranch. He'd only ridden a few hundred yards, but it was lost in the dark and blowing snow. How many trees had he passed already? Was this a sign? Only one way to find out, he thought, as he spurred Mackie forward to the next tree. Nothing. He crossed the lane and checked trees there.

Nothing. Back to the right side of the trail and more trees. Nothing. What else could it be but a sign? He rode on and saw the next hacked scar before he got to it, the raw wound glowed against the dark trunk in the night sky nearly as much as the snow itself.

He pulled off a mitten and ran his fingers over the gash, squinting at it in the harsh wind and dim light. It was made by a large knife, but not an ax, he didn't think. The edges of each bite appeared too narrow. It looked like it was made by a flat, long blade. A long Bowie knife, a machete, or sword. He sat up, pulling on his mitten. So it was now a fact. The barefoot gypsy man wore that large knife sheathed about his waist. And what's more, he wanted him to follow. Expected him to. There could be but one reason: he wanted something Niall had. He took Jenna, probably only as bait to lure Niall out here. It didn't make a heck of a lot of sense yet. But at least now he had a trail to follow.

It must be the gypsy man, he was a hard case. But the woman, she might be innocent. Niall would give them that much. But what did they want? The house was gone through, their possessions tossed every which way. It was likely that items were stolen, though what they might be, he had no idea, but it was more than just his wife they wanted, for they already had her.

He refused to believe they killed her and that she lay somewhere about the ranch, undiscovered by him in the dark. He had searched everywhere he could think of. He drove this vile thought from his mind and spurred the black horse, plunging ahead on the trail, into the forest, keeping a sharp eye for scarred trees.

11

In the dark, the horse slid down a gravel ravine and faltered. No matter how much Greasy tried to get it moving again, it just wouldn't budge. Damn thing had never been too reliable. He slid off and slapped the beast open-handed on the rump. He punched it in the side, nothing got it motivated. Then without warning the horse slumped forward onto its front knees. It swayed like that and Greasy, shivering and jaws chattering, said, 'Oh no you don't. Don't you do this to me!' The wind whipped his voice away.

It was evident that he was not going to raise the horse from its knees, and indeed it would probably continue its decline until it was flat on the ground. So Greasy tugged on the cinch and tried to get the saddle off the horse before it continued its inevitable fall. It didn't work. The horse swayed then flopped against the gravel bank, its feet sticking out in a tangle, twitching. He kicked at the horse, yelling and shaking his hands at the sky. 'Why me?' he shouted. 'Why? What did I do to deserve this?' With every kick the horse flinched less and less.

Greasy finally climbed up above it on the bank and pulled at the saddle until it came free. Other than the horse it was the only thing of any value he owned. He dragged it up away from the horse and with a final kick that caught the horse on a jutting hip bone, he pulled the saddle up the bank and stood squinting into the dark.

They had spun several times before tumbling down the slight ravine and now he couldn't tell which way to head. He could push forward, to meet the stranger on the trail. Question was, which way was forward? And where was the trail? That stranger must be somewhere nearby and hunkered down for the night. If he was headed where

Greasy thought, considering his questions of yesterday, then he might already be there.

Greasy faced into the blowing snow and squinted. If I don't make a decision soon, then I'm going to be dead where I stand. I can't go back, so I better move in some direction, try to locate the stranger. He regretted even leaving town, but it was too late. If he lived through the storm, then he would have to head back to town, take his licks, and maybe get his job back at the saloon. Cornell Waite was a pushover. Greasy knew he could make the old man feel guilty about leaving him jobless, and in cold weather, too.

He shivered and stamped his feet hard, dropped the saddle, and thrust his bare hands up under his arms. He had relied on the whiskey he had taken from Winters' place for warmth. It was now gone and he was colder than he remembered ever feeling. The snow was halfway up his boots and showing no signs of slowing down. He squinted into the cursed wind-driven snow. Was it coming from the east or west before they toppled? The wind seemed to come from every direction here in the trees. He realized as he turned around, not able to see very far in any direction, that he was lost. He bent close to the ground to locate their tracks coming in. He walked around the gully, but he couldn't see them. He looked down below him at the big unmoving shape of his horse, now barely visible, half-covered with snow. 'What am I gonna do now?'

He went back to his saddle and pad and hefted it up over his head, covering his shoulders, the stirrups clunking him on the arms. He chose a direction and set off, hoping it would lead toward the stranger. At least when he walked the cold wasn't so bad. His hands and ears still ached and the top of his buckskin shirt wouldn't stay pulled up over his mouth and nose. His feet were so cold he couldn't even feel them anymore. He trudged through the snow on what looked a bit like a path, wishing with each step he was back at the saloon. Even if it meant sweeping the floor and dumping spittoons.

*   *   *

It seemed to Greasy he'd been walking for days when he thought he saw a light. It couldn't be, of course. Not out here. He gave up miles ago on ever living through the storm, but he figured he might as well walk while he could. You never know, he told himself. That was his mother's favorite saying. But she must have known. A drunkard for a husband and a drunkard for a son. Where was she now? Still in St. Louis? Still alive? He was a long way from home. He'd always meant to get back there to see her. Now he never would get the chance. Just as well. It wasn't like they'd parted on good terms.

And then he saw a flash of light, warm and orange, like a candle far away. A struck match, maybe? He fixed the point as best he could and trudged toward it. What did it matter now? Might as well see if there's anything to it. Die in the trees over there as easy as over here.

He saw the light once more, another brief offering, to the right of where he was headed. He altered course, the barest flicker of promise kindling in his near-cold breast. Within minutes he walked into the side of some sort of structure. It was blowing so hard he couldn't tell quite what it was, but he smelled wood smoke and then he felt a wheel with his hands.

'Hello!' he shouted. He dropped his saddle. The pad slipped from his shoulders, but he didn't care. There was someone in there, someone who had a warm fire going. He walked around the thing, might be a wagon, pounding weakly on the sides. 'Hello? Hello?' He tripped over the traces at the front and made his way around the far side. Here he was almost cut off from the wind and snow. It was a relief, and then he walked right into something large and hairy. It snorted at him and he steadied his heart — it was just a horse. But small, at that. Unless it was standing in a hole. Nope, just small. Maybe a pony.

He ducked under its tether and made his way around to what must be the back of the wagon, feeling the wood sides, slapping them and saying, 'Hello! Hello in there!' He was regaining a bit of his strength, but as he came around the corner the wind hit him again. He felt the side of a door, and then his toes clunked against a step. He hammered on the door with a fist and yelled again, louder than before. He slapped the wood, groping for a handle, and found a steel loop with a thumb latch. He tried it, but it was locked from the inside.

'Please, please let me in. I'll die out here. Please help me!' He pounded on the door again. He thought he heard a dog bark and then the latch rattled. The door opened and that warm glow he saw earlier greeted him. A face stared at him from the sliver of light. He wiped at his eyes and leaned closer. A dog growled somewhere within. Did he know who this was? Out here? He still wasn't convinced it was a real wagon with a real pony and real wood smoke, let alone knowing who it might be out here in the middle of nowhere.

'What do you want?' said the face in a stern voice and Greasy knew in an instant who it was: the gypsies. He saw the man's big moustache now, the angry eyes. Would he remember Greasy and how he had treated them? The things he said about them?

He bent his head down. 'I need help. I'm gonna die out here. Please help me.' Greasy put his hands together and held them up in front of his face.

The man disappeared and the gap of light narrowed, though it did not close all the way. The man's face appeared again, still looking angry, but he pulled the door open and said, 'Come in now. Hurry, hurry.'

Greasy shook snow from his hat and

shoulders then climbed into the little heated wagon. He closed the door behind him and as he turned to face the gypsies he heard a gasp and the man said, 'You!' And in a flash the man's long knife pointed at Greasy's gut.

12

'Now, now look,' said Greasy, still shivering. 'I ain't myself. I'm cold. I don't want no trouble.'

'If I had known it was you I would not have let you in.' The man's dark eyes glared at Greasy and a set of strong, white teeth gritted together beneath the massive moustache. The woman stood behind the man, tight-lipped and staring with the same dark, piercing eyes. She held back a growling black and white collie, muzzle gone gray. The dog's eyes were clouded but its lips quivered high over bared yellow teeth. Despite these dangers, the heavenly smell of turkey meat boiling on the stove filled him with hope.

'Please just let me get warm. I won't cause no harm. I'm so cold.' And his mouth chattered in emphasis. 'And hungry.'

The man stared at him, still holding the knife, then said, 'Sit there,' pointing to a small built-in bench by the little glowing stove. 'And do not move.'

Greasy did so and for the next ten minutes nothing more was said. His buckskins steamed and as the heat worked into his raw, red hands he pulled them back from nearly touching the top of the stove. The dog stopped growling as long as the old woman stroked its muzzle. Greasy decided it was blind, but far from harmless. The old couple stared at him, unmasked hatred in their eyes. Greasy tried to keep his gaze from meeting theirs. Finally he said, 'I didn't mean nothing I said in town. I was showboatin' for my friends, you know?'

'Are you warm?' said the man, the hint of a smile on his mouth.

'Yessir, I feel much better,' said Greasy.

The man's smile faded and he said, 'Then get out.' And he pointed to the door with his knife.

151

'You can't mean that.' Greasy looked from one to the other. They were unchanging. 'I would die out there.'

The dog resumed growling. The woman's face, while still stern, was not as set as her husband's, Greasy could see a bit of hope there. But the old man was dead set on putting him out, there was no hope on his face. He hated that face. So high and mighty. And Greasy decided right then and there what he would do. He would not get angry. But he would not be put out in the cold, either.

He stood slowly, stretching. 'All right,' he said, looking at them with eyes as sad as he could make them. He turned to the door and put a hand on the latch. 'All right, I'm going.' He opened the door wide, turned and said, 'Thank you for your hospitality.' He set a foot on the first step and saw the man move to close the door. He moved forward another step and when the door was almost closed he slammed all his weight back

152

against it with his shoulder.

As the door pushed inward, the knife clattered to the floor and Greasy saw the old man stumble and fall into the woman, the dog, confused, squirmed beneath them yelping. The woman screamed. Greasy shot forward on all fours and grabbed the old man's knife near their scrambling feet. As his hand closed around the handle the man shouted, 'No!'

Before Greasy could get to his feet the old man lunged at him. Greasy held the knife up and the old man walked right into it. Just like Drift, thought Greasy, fascinated, as he watched the knife's blade disappear into the old man's shirt.

Greasy pulled on the knife and held it out, dark red blood dripping from the tip. The old man fell to his knees, clutching his gut. He made a grunting noise and sounded short of breath. The dog clawed its way from between the man and woman and leapt at Greasy, its throat colliding with his forearm, the dulled teeth tearing his cheek open. He arched the knife and slammed it hard into the dog's ribcage. The dog's cloudy eyes flew open wide and a final breath caught Greasy full in the face before the animal sagged motionless on top of him. The old lady kept screaming and held her husband by the shoulders. He flopped to his side on the floor, curled up and holding his belly. She leaned over him, crying and cooing.

'Shut up!' yelled Greasy, pointing the knife at the woman. He was breathing heavy and stood over her. The blood dripped on her dress and she crawled close to her husband, curling her legs around him.

He grabbed the dog by the scruff and flung it out the door. Turning back inside, Greasy looked down at the whimpering woman and saw a band of skin between the top of her mess of socks and the bottom of some pants she was wearing under her skirts. He narrowed his eyes and looked at her. She wasn't all that old. He ran his tongue over his lips and reached behind him, slamming closed the door. The woman looked up at him, eyes wide, and he smiled down at her.

13

The stranger toed the bottoms of Jenna's boots. Her eyes popped open. It was still dark when he woke her. It had grown colder, the singular cold that comes creeping in the early hours before dawn. Unlike the warm, comforting feeling of waking beside Niall, when she was always a little disoriented for the first few seconds of her day, she awakened here against the tree fully and in an instant. She knew her situation, recalled everything of the day before and waited, tense, until he came to untie her. She must have slept well, if not for long, for she felt her strength somewhat restored.

Though it stormed most of the previous afternoon and evening, she was still surprised to find herself covered with a good six inches of dense snow. And it was still coming down.

He untied the ropes from her waist and feet. Then he pointed to just behind the tree and said, 'Do what you need to. We're leavin'.' She stood and stretched, working her legs and feet, arching her back. He had the horses saddled and loaded, and he stood by them, adjusting straps, his back to her. She took his advice and when through worked the blanket tight about her head and shoulders and gripped it tight from the inside with her hands. She prayed he wouldn't take it from her.

Leaning against her horse, she put her left foot into the stirrup and tried to grab the pommel and still retain her grip on the blanket, which she knew would be crucial as the day progressed. It still smelled like snow and she was sure it would continue well into today. She was halfway up onto Sweet Baby and without having two independent arms to help pull herself, she couldn't make it up and over with her right leg. He walked back and put a hand to her waist, roughly pushing her upward.

Once she was in the saddle his hand rested on her thigh longer than necessary. She looked down at the top of his hat and jerked her leg as if shooing a fly. He let his hand fall and so quick she didn't see the movement, he reached up and yanked the edge of the wool blanket with such force it whipped from her shoulders and flew from her clenched hands.

'No, please!' she cried. He walked away, rolling the blanket, and stuffing it under two straps on Slate, the pack horse.

Jenna sank in a moment of hopelessness. But as she watched him mount up, her hatred for him flamed. She thought that the dark coat and the dirty black hat didn't look so very big. He seemed, if anything, to have diminished somehow since yesterday. She thought of Niall, so strong and kind, and for the first time since her ordeal began she felt a sense of power. Slight, to be sure, but it was enough at that moment.

As they left the clearing for the trail,

he stopped and in the same gesture she had seen countless times the day before, he pulled out the machete and hacked a mark into a tree. These marks, she knew, were meant for Niall. And while she hoped he hurried, she also hoped he used more caution than he ever had before.

14

Daylight seeped in so gradually that Niall rode for nearly an hour before he realized he was once again seeing the rough trail rather than sensing it by the snow's dull glow. The sky was close and thick like mattress ticking and of such a deep gray he was surprised any light made its way through at all. It was so close it looked as if he could touch it with the tip of his rifle barrel, in its sheath by his left knee. During the night the wind had lessened, though the snow continued and, judging from the tang in the air, today would be another day of steady falling snow.

The light nudged certain familiar landmarks on the horizon into view. Shiller's Peak, the largest and most commanding, lay just to the north, though he hadn't been this far up in five or so years, a good while after the end of the range war. There hadn't been a need. Any further and he'd raise painful old memories that were best left dead. But now he had no choice.

In following the gypsy's blatant trail, Niall deviated from the old roadway in the night. He hadn't expected them to take to the trees with that wagon and two horses in tow but he was pleased to note the fault of the old man's decision. It meant that he'd come upon them soon. With the snow he expected to accumulate throughout the coming day, Niall doubted that little gypsy pony would make it much further. The terrain was growing less forgiving, too. The rolling landscape of the foothills gave way to steeper, rocky trails riddled with jagged outcroppings half-hidden in drifted snow. The trees, while still numerous, would soon become gnarled and bent, and like every living thing in the mountains, their time here was spent fighting for survival.

Niall guided Mackie slowly through the deepening snow. Any amount of haste could result in the horse putting a foot wrong, a dire possibility at the best of times. Niall kept his squinted gaze fixed on the trail ahead and the less numerous markings of the gypsy. All of Niall's face but his eyes was hidden beneath an ample kerchief wrapped tight. He gave thanks once again to Jenna who made his rabbit fur hat with skins she'd saved from his hunting forays. She'd made one for Uncle Drift as well, though to Niall's knowledge he never wore it. He claimed he was keeping it for best.

The devil's in the details, Niall. Drift's favorite phrase rang in his head. The further Niall rode from what remained of his ranch, the more he thought of those very first months spent married to Jenna, by far the sweetest days of his life. Not that the subsequent years hadn't been just fine, but there was something special about those first few months, that first year of their marriage. Drift had cut them a wide trail then, knowing as all good friends do, that the lopsided loyalties were due only to the change Niall's life had taken.

And knowing Drift as he did, Niall was sure the old coot knew that their lives would sort themselves out and all would be as it had been, but with an added element that they both knew Niall had needed for years. But now that Niall thought back on that time, for the first time he admitted that they both seemed strange to him then, just after the range war had ended. He thought it a matter of everything in their lives changing — the war, the ranch, their new marriage — that it had come out in them in those little moments of quiet, the exchanged looks.

Niall shook his head and frowned at himself. How could he think this way? And about the two people who meant the most to him? There could be no doubt she was completely devoted to him. He never questioned that, and indeed their lives had grown strong and fine in the intervening years. The three of them were as close as any people could be without being blood related. Niall remarked to her once that they were probably closer than blood relatives because they chose each other. She gave him a look so odd that he wished he hadn't given voice to the thought.

Mackie slowed and nickered and Niall shook himself out of his reverie and cursed out loud for not paying attention in the saddle, ignoring the fact that he'd been without sleep for more than a day. He detested lack of mindfulness in others and he certainly wouldn't tolerate it in himself. Mackie nickered again and through the snowfall Niall was startled to see, not fifty feet ahead of him, the familiar painted wagon of the gypsies.

* * *

It was canted at an odd angle, close to a thick spruce. The pony was nowhere to be seen and the wagon was buried to its axles in solid snow. It had been there all night. Niall sat still, the only movement his and the horse's breath rising on the cold morning air. Something was off with this situation, and it bothered him that he couldn't tell what it was. While he kept his gaze on the little wagon, he pulled his Winchester from its cowhide sheath, levered, checked it, and unfastened the buttons on his coat, wedging it back behind his holster. He urged Mackie forward another twenty feet, then stopped.

'You in the wagon. Come on out. I know you're in there.'

No answer. Had they abandoned the wagon and gone ahead on horseback? They did have Slate, Sweet Baby, and their pony. A finger of wind blew snow crystals across the morning sun's rays from a cluster of nearby spruce. He squeezed his eyes shut tight for a second to melt the crystals on his eyelashes, then forced them wide. Nothing had changed. He looked upslope for sign of movement, in the direction he likely would have followed had the wagon not been there. It could be a trap to lure him into the little clearing in the trees. He looked in every direction and could see no sign of anyone or anything that shouldn't be there.

'What do you say, Mackie?' Niall had grown to trust an animal's instincts in addition to his own in certain situations. And this one fit the bill. But Mackie wasn't bothered since his initial sighting of the wagon. Niall sighed and with his rifle shouldered, he urged Mackie in behind the wagon, keeping the narrowest part of it dead in front of him.

He came to within twenty feet of the little door and dismounted by a dead-fall, skeletal branches poking through the otherwise untouched surface of the snow. Without taking his eyes from the little door, he looped Mackie's reins around a thick branch and stepped high through the snow until he reached the back of the wagon.

'In the wagon! Come on out!' He waited a moment, then poked the faded little door with the end of the rifle. Nothing. He turned his body to the side and reached for the latch, keeping the rifle cradled and aiming at the door. It swung inward. The little interior was dark. Niall stood to one side of the door and squinted in. At first he saw nothing, then he made out the bottoms of a pair of bare feet, hard and dirty, facing him.

He kept low and moved closer, peering in at floor level. There was no movement. Was the man dead? He poked his rifle in, tapping a calloused foot. No response. He put a foot on the one step and the wagon creaked and sank with his weight. And then he heard a gasp from within. He stepped back and pulled the rifle to his shoulder and again from within the wagon came a gasp, then a sob.

'Who's there?' he said. The crying grew louder. It was a woman. 'Jenna?' but he knew it wasn't her.

'Please, no more. Please. I tell you we have no gold,' said a woman's voice. The old gypsy woman.

He stepped closer and still holding up the rifle, said, 'What's happened here? Where are you?'

A rustling, then a scraping sound, and she crawled toward the door. She held a knife in one hand, clunking it against the floor as she crawled. She held the other hand to her chest, her weight resting forward on the hand with the knife.

As soon as he saw her face he knew he must be wrong. Whoever killed Drift and stole Jenna probably attacked these people. But who? And why?

Thick purple and black bruises puffed her cheeks and one side of her face. Her top lip was split and dried blood trailed from her nostrils.

'Who did this?' he said, leaning the rifle against the wagon.

She looked up at him and pulled back, clutching the knife. There was animal fear in her eyes. 'Ma'am,' he said in a slow, even voice, 'is your husband dead?'

She just stared at him and said, 'Go away now! No more!'

He realized he still had his kerchief pulled up over his face and his hat pulled down low on his brow. He pulled the kerchief down and pushed his hat back a bit. 'Do you recognize me, ma'am? I talked with you back in town yesterday.'

He saw the fear drain from her face and she dropped the knife.

He remounted the step and knelt just inside the wagon. He gently touched her shoulder. She flinched and pulled away. 'Ma'am, I can help you. What happened here?' He turned to the old man, lying on his back beside her. 'Is he . . . is your husband dead?'

She cried out and fell forward across the old man's legs, crying. Niall pushed the knife out of her reach and knelt there by the old man's bare feet, not knowing what to do, and cursing himself for thinking that he would now be saddled with this woman and no extra mount and no way to push on and find Jenna.

As she wept, clutching at her husband's pant legs, the old man's feet moved. Niall thought it was because of her, but he couldn't be sure. He gently pulled her off him and leaned over the man. He pulled back a blanket and looked close. He'd been stabbed in the gut and his clothes were soaked through.

Niall leaned over the man and though the woman's sobs filled the little space he heard ragged breath. It was faint but it was there. It was too dark to tell by sight if the old man's chest was actually rising and falling with the act of breathing.

He sat up and took her by the shoulders. 'Ma'am, I need you to calm down and listen to me. He's alive. But I don't know if he'll live much longer if we don't warm him up and dress his wound.'

The little wagon, now that he could

see in the darkened interior, was a little home on wheels. But it was a mess with their meager possessions strewn everywhere. Forward was a double bunk, small, but then they weren't large people. The rest was filled with cabinets and cupboards, and a space for a fold-down table. Off to the left, the smallest woodstove he ever saw. He touched it, cold.

Niall hated to move the man, but it would be better for him to be up on the bunk than on the cold floor. He looked at the old woman but she still wasn't responding. 'Ma'am, we've all been through a rough time here but if we don't do something about it things are gonna get rougher before too long.'

That seemed to make a difference. She stopped crying and now looked at him. He lifted the old man with as much care as he knew how, all the while thinking of Drift and how much heavier he had been when he had moved him in the barn. When had that been? Just last night? It seemed years ago.

The old man groaned. That got her attention. 'We need to get him to bed,' said Niall. 'Smooth that bedding and pull back that top covering.' He knew if he didn't tend to the man right away he might lose him, though he probably would die anyway. A gut wound was usually fatal. And a slow way to die. Yesterday at the store the man was so alive with defiance and pride, the swarthy features and skin dark like tanned leather, but now he was relaxed in unconsciousness. He hadn't dressed a wound like this since The War Between the States. Then there had been plenty of bayonet wounds to go around.

'Will this work?' He pointed to the little stove. She nodded, pulling up the soiled quilt from the floor. He looked at it and then at her. He hadn't noticed before but it was just like the blanket on his and Jenna's bed. She saw him, but turned to cover her husband.

Niall stepped down, out into the snow. They were in a glade, though because of the numerous surrounding trees they were somewhat protected by the wind, which was once again picking up. Mackie, still tied to the deadfall, didn't seem to mind that they stopped. It was a long night and the interruption would be good for both of them. He snapped light, dry, and dead branches where they grew in profusion off the lower trunks of the thick pines. The deadfall would provide larger wood. He retied Mackie to the wagon's rear wheel and dragged wood close to the wagon, then brought in his rifle along with the wood.

Due to the stove's size, the wood had to be snapped into small pieces in order to fit, but within a few minutes he had a fire going. It wouldn't take much to heat such a small space, and he was glad for it. They'd need to warm the old man and boil some water, clean him up so Niall could take a look at the wound, see what they were dealing with. The old woman had been treated pretty hard, he didn't know just how badly, but she was pretty shaken up. He guessed the abuse to her face wasn't all she had undergone. And his insides knotted at the thought that, at best Jenna was with the devil who had done this. At worst . . . He put it from his mind and concentrated on the task at hand.

Within a half-hour he had the wagon warmed, got their oil lantern lit, and had cleaned up the old man as best he could. The water was not quite hot but it would do for now. The old man would live, Niall felt, if an infection didn't set in. He ripped into strips the skirting from a dress she gave him, and wrapped the wound as best he could to keep it tight and clean.

Niall left her to tend him and he cleaned up the mess in the wagon. Whoever did this ransacked the little home from front to back.

The old woman sat beside her husband, whispering close to his ear, kissing his forehead. Niall left them and went outside to Mackie. He measured

174

out a double helping of corn and tied on the horse's feed bag, took off the saddle and saddle bags, and rubbed down the big horse with the rough saddle blanket, then went over him again with a few handfuls of pine needles he stripped off low branches.

Mackie nickered and leaned against him. It had been a long ride and Niall was sure they had much further to go. It would do the horse good to have this bit of rest. As he rubbed him down he looked around, but he was sure that whoever did this had moved on. But where? He doubted they were waiting for him, doubted they did this to trap him here, otherwise they would have fired on him by now.

There were no tracks leading out of here. The constant snow did a thorough job in covering any sign. He only hoped he hadn't lost the slashed tree trail in the night. He looked toward where the land sloped uphill. Though he couldn't see much beyond the trees shrouding the little glade, he knew what lay beyond. How anyone could know of that place was beyond him, that lonely place up there in those rocks. If they headed in that direction they might pass by it and never know it existed. He hoped that would be the case.

He slung his saddle-bags over his shoulder and knocked on the little door, then entered. It was warm and lit by the lantern oil's glow. She was in the same position, crouched over her husband, smoothing his hair, and whispering to him. Niall stayed to the rear of the wagon and unpacked his saddle bags. His rations were meager but they would have to do.

He melted enough snow to fill his coffeepot, then unwrapped the biscuits and jerked meat. He dumped loose coffee into the pot and waited for it to boil. In a little while he handed her a cup of coffee. She didn't want to take it, didn't want to leave her husband's side.

'Ma'am, if you don't drink and eat you'll be no better off than him. He needs you to be strong for him right now.' He paused, then said, 'I can't stay. I'll be back for you, but right now I have to push on.'

Her eyes grew wide when he said this. The fear from before creeping back in. 'I'll not let them come back,' he offered. They both sipped in silence. He offered her a biscuit and ate one himself.

'My wife made these.' He looked at her. She didn't look at him. 'Ma'am, you know why I'm out here. Someone has kidnapped my wife, burned my place, and killed my Uncle Drift.' He felt his throat tighten, his anger rise and constrict in his throat. He sipped his coffee and said, 'I know you were there. I need you to tell me and who did this. What were they like? Did you see if my wife was with them? She's a young woman, dark hair, long, though she often wears it up. She's very pretty.'

The old woman looked at him now and said, 'No. No one was with him.'

Her mouth trembled but she continued, 'It was the man from town. The one who said those things.' She turned to her husband. 'I told him to leave the man alone. There would be trouble, but my husband . . . ' She turned to Niall. 'My husband is a proud man.'

'The man he argued with in the street?' said Niall. She nodded. That would have been Greasy. He knew Greasy was an unsavory character, but to have done this? 'Was he alone?'

Again, she nodded. None of this made sense. He thought over his visit to town, his conversation with the Dibbses, seeing the gypsy man in the store, what Greasy said of gypsies and bad luck. If what she said was true, then Greasy was the bad luck, not these people.

'He said we had gold, but we have no gold. How could we?' she held her hands out, palms up, and looked about the cramped little wagon.

Niall nodded and said, 'How did you come to be up here in the mountains so late in the season?'

The old woman looked at him with liquid eyes as if deciding something, then looked at her husband, whose breathing had settled into a recognizable rhythm, and said, 'We were very far to the south, grazing our flock. We were near a town and my husband walked into town for . . . ' She said a word he didn't know and waved her hand at his saddle-bag.

'Supplies? Food and such?'

She nodded and continued, 'It was late and he did not come back. And that night they stole our sheep. I could not stop them. Our dog tried but . . . ' She held up her hands in futility. 'We did not have many sheep, but they were enough for us.'

Niall had forgotten about the dog he had heard barking inside their wagon in town. 'Where is your dog now?'

'Those thieves in that town shot her. She was in the wagon, getting well, but last night . . . ' She raised her broken hand to her forehead to cover her eyes.

'She is outside.'

So Greasy had killed an old, injured dog, too.

'And your pony?' Niall almost hated to ask.

'He stole him.'

From behind her came a gasp and a whispered word. It was the old man. She bent over him. Niall moved closer. The old man whispered something to his wife in their native language and she nodded. 'He is thirsty,' she whispered.

Niall had torn bits of jerky and soaked them in a cup of hot water. 'Tell him not to overdo it. A little at a time. This will help build his strength up. You'll have to keep doing this. And you should eat, too.' He addressed the woman, though he knew the man was now awake. He could see his open eyes in the dim light.

'So how did that get you up this far into such mountainous country?' Niall asked, as she helped her husband to drink.

She said nothing. The old man spoke.

It was a weak, raspy sound, but Niall could hear him. 'We followed them. Too late, they sold our sheep, the ones they did not kill. I followed them for too long and now — ' His voice broke off.

'You wanted to catch the person who stole your sheep. I can understand that,' he said, feeling the urge to leave, to track Greasy and find out what was going on, why strangers were in the mountains behind his house thicker than cattle on a drive. And why so much trouble came with them. Then he remembered something Bert Dibbs said. He'd paid it no mind at the time, something about a stranger riding through, when was it? A day or two ago? He cursed himself for not asking more questions. Had Greasy been in cahoots with the stranger? He should have asked. He should have . . . He stopped himself. That sort of thinking would get him nowhere.

'What were they like? The people who stole your sheep?'

She shook her head and said, 'They

181

are gone a long time now. On a train. But we had nowhere to go. We are mountain people.' She glanced at her husband. 'We thought maybe these mountains . . . '

'Ma'am, I don't know what the mountains are like where you come from but here they're unforgiving half of the year and pretty rough the rest of the time. It's the winters, as you can see, that will get to you. Soon these mountains will be blocked with snow for the next six, seven months.'

She nodded in understanding. 'We went to that town.'

'Where I met you, yes, that's Dibbston.'

She laid a hand on her husband's and said, 'He looked at the blankets but — '

'Too much money?' said Niall, refilling his cup.

'I was going to take one from that store but I could not,' said the old man. 'I felt that everything people here has said about us is all true.'

'That is not true!' his wife said. 'You

182

have never been a thief in your life!'

He looked up at her. 'That is not true. I stole from you. I stole your youth and happiness.'

She called him something in their language and kissed him on the forehead.

'You should keep quiet now. Try to sleep,' said Niall.

Moments later, assured that her husband was once again asleep, the old woman touched the blanket covering him and said, 'We took from you. You know this.' She looked right at Niall.

'I did invite you to stop, you remember. I would guess that you were cold and the house was empty and open. And when you found no one there, you took a blanket. I hope you took some food, too. I wish you had just stayed there, though. You would have been better off.'

She shook her head. 'We were afraid. We did not dare to go back. After we left your house, we followed an old road but became lost in the snow.'

Niall nodded. 'You didn't see anyone at my place? No sign of anyone?'

'No. We were too scared. Bad things happened there. We should have gone back to the town.' She looked over her shoulder at her husband, 'But we went on.'

'You didn't go in the barn?'

She looked down, closing her eyes tight.

'He was already dead,' she said in a whisper.

Niall fought back an unquenchable anger. It was not their fault. The worst thing they'd done was to come along the wrong place at the wrong time. And then things got even worse for them.

'You said your dog is outside?'

She nodded. 'She is under the wagon. In the snow. I covered her.' The woman's eyes brightened and she said, 'Bella fought him. She hurt his face. I saw this.' She touched her own face and winced at the tenderness there.

'We should tend to your hand and your face. Soak that hand in hot water.

We'll see what sort of sling we can rig up.'

She touched his sleeve. 'Thank you so well for helping us.'

He patted her hand and said, 'It's just fine, ma'am. Glad I could do it, is all.'

One finger was swollen and bent. He helped to wrap her hand and tie it in a sling.

'I am Zell, not ma'am. My husband is Rudolfo.' She smiled at him weakly as he finished tying the sling.

'Pleased to know that, ma'am, uh, Zell.' He smiled. 'I'm Niall. Niall Winters.'

'Your wife?'

His smile faded. 'She's Jenna.'

I've been here long enough, he thought. I have to move on.

'Zell, I have to go now. I've been here for a couple of hours. I've stacked plenty of wood inside for you and there's enough water on the stove for a while yet. Melt snow if you need more.' He unloaded his saddle-bags and took a biscuit and a few strips of jerky. The rest he left for her. They would need it to build up their strength. He could shoot a rabbit, maybe even a mountain sheep on the trail, if need be.

He slung his saddle bag over his shoulder, pulled on his mittens and picked up his rifle. 'You'll need to keep him from moving. Feed him that broth and keep this wagon warm. If you need more wood, I've stacked another pile just outside. I have to go. But I'll be back.'

He stepped outside and saddled Mackie. As he climbed up into the saddle, she said, 'I pray for you and for your wife, Niall Winters.'

He nodded to her and reined Mackie back out toward the trail.

As he rode out of the little glade, her thank yous still fresh in his ears, he thought that he'd need a lot more than prayers to help him now. I'm heading into a little bit of hell, he thought.

15

The throbbing in Jenna's hands kept her from falling asleep, though she hoped it was only sleep that pulled at her, forcing her head to slump forward. She had been so cold since they started that morning, well before dawn. He had taken her blanket and now she felt nothing more than numb, the occasional twinge of sharp pain jarring her when her horse stepped hard, which happened with more frequency now that they were heading up into the rocky hills.

The wind, in sudden bursts, whipped the tree branches, with random gusts slicing through at ground level. The sky had darkened early and through it all the snow continued falling, thick and heavy. Her fingers grew so numb she could no longer grip with them and her shawl slipped off her shoulders before she realized what happened. One end of it dragged on the ground behind, the other end still caught in the crook of her arm. 'Help!' she yelled, but he never even turned to acknowledge her plea.

A few minutes later the trailing shawl snagged on a finger of rock, pulled, and slipped from her arm. 'I need help!' she yelled, her teeth chattering. 'My shawl has slipped off. I'm freezing.' The black coat and hat never shifted position, the roan continued picking its way upward through sparse evergreens.

She knew the man heard her. She would have cursed at him, but she was so cold she could think of nothing but sitting close by her cookstove on a cold winter night with Niall and Drift, sipping coffee and talking. Snow pelted down, touching her cheeks, her eyelashes, but for just a moment she was home again with her family, all whole and safe.

She knew she would never see Drift alive again. Would she also never see her husband? Never feel his strong arms hold her tight to him? As if in response, her gaze fell on Slate, Niall's big gray, tethered between her and the stranger and used as a pack horse. She fancied the horse was embarrassed by this turn of fortunes. In this cold and without Niall astride him he looked like just another horse clumping his way over an unforgiving landscape.

A few minutes later, though as cold as she was it could have been days later, he pulled up short and leaned forward, peering uphill through the snow to his right at the tangle of viney growth that covered the rocky face above them.

A strange sensation of familiarity struck Jenna again, so much so that she shook her head to help clear her thoughts. Surely this couldn't be the place. It had been eight years, but this was too small, too close. Everything looked different covered with snow. If she ever was here, she reasoned, she wasn't sure she'd now recognize it with this layer of snow over everything.

He dismounted and climbed over

and around a few boulders, heading toward the matted tangle of vegetation draped over the rock face above. He turned back just once, and drawing the machete he pointed it straight at her and shook it once for emphasis. Then he turned and worked his way over the rocks, heading up the last twenty feet to the top, gravel and small rocks sliding with the snow under his boots.

She sat on Sweet Baby, taking his gesture as a warning against escape. Well, he's safe on that point, she thought. There's no way I'm going anywhere. I can't feel most of my body for the cold, my horse is tethered to two other horses, and my hands are still bound where he tied the rope to the saddle horn. She wished he had at least kept them loose so she could help herself maintain balance in the saddle. It was difficult, especially when they left the shelter of the trees behind and headed into the rougher, ragged trails of the low peaks.

He reached the wall of stringy

vegetation and poked the blade straight into it several times. She was surprised to see the blade sink in to the hilt. Then without hesitation he hacked at it with the machete. She expected to hear the sudden noise of steel scraping stone, but, as he pulled away slashed and broken vines, an ever-growing blackness before him revealed itself as the mouth of a cave. The cave.

In the time it takes for a long-buried memory to surface whole as if waiting for her, she knew that they had reached it. She trembled all over now, and not from the cold.

No, she thought in defiance. I am wrong. It's the cold and the snow playing tricks on me. But still she shook her head and struggled in vain with her bonds, chafing into bleeding her already raw wrists. But she never felt the pain. This place represented something far worse to her. Something more terrible than mere physical pain. She knew only too intimately what lay in that cave and worse, what had happened in that cave eight years before. And at the same time of year. The situation was nearly identical. She closed her eyes and fought to bring her breathing under control.

But some things are different. I am not the same person I was all those years ago. I could never be that same carefree girl again. She let her head fall forward, her shoulders slump. Too much had been stripped away from her in that cave. And now she was here once more. Back at a place she swore she would never again see. Niall had promised her that. And she had believed him. But here she was and he was nowhere in sight.

She was sure she would never see him again. And as she clenched her jaw tight, fighting back tears, she worked to control her breathing and then she felt a firm grip on her forearm and he was there. She blinked hard twice and her vision cleared and it was the bad man untying the rope from the saddle horn. He grabbed the rope between her hands and pulled her roughly.

She managed to land on her right foot before collapsing to her knee, struggling to get her other foot underneath herself. She was nearly upright when he pulled her again and she fell into line roughly behind him. Her wet, matted hair hung in her eyes. He tugged her like a calf on a lead line over rocks and up the twenty-foot talus slope toward the cave. They were halfway up, navigating silent gray boulders, when she stiffened, shouting a ragged 'No!'

She pulled back on the rope and without warning he was above her. His left hand lashed out, catching her full across the face. His face was less than an inch from hers and he looked down at her, his hat tilted back just enough so that she could again see his eyes. She knew she had been lying to herself since yesterday. She also now knew without doubt who he was. And she screamed.

★ ★ ★

She did not fight him the rest of the way up the slope to the cave. He pushed her head down hard with a firm hand, forcing her to bend low to step through the opening. Once inside she remembered that she could stand full height. His height kept him in a crouch. He waited for their eyes to adjust to the dim light and then pushed her further into the cave. She crouched down and stepped forward with caution, unsure of the walls and floor. He spun her around, grabbed the hand rope again and forced her down to the sandy floor. 'Sit,' he said.

She leaned against the rock wall as he tied her feet and tested the rope around her wrists. He left the cave. For a moment she felt panic flare in her. He was leaving her here to die alone in this place. Think, she told herself. He wouldn't bring you all the way here to leave you. He might if he wasn't real.

She argued back and forth with herself this way, too exhausted to care much one way or another. She forced herself to look around the gloom of the cave. There was nothing in it, as she remembered, except for that pile of rocks, beyond her, in the back of the cave.

She groped the sandy floor with her fingers for a sharp rock so she might work away at the ropes on her wrists and found nothing but a bit of ancient, dried stick that crumbled in her grasp. She gritted her teeth and refused to give in to despair. Niall would not behave this way in such a situation and from what Uncle Drift had told her, he and Niall had been in plenty of tough spots in his life before he met her.

Niall always turned the conversation from such topics whenever she tried to raise them early on in their marriage. It didn't take her long to figure out that he didn't want to talk about such things any more than she would want to talk about what had happened in this very cave all those years ago.

She heard boots on the rocks outside the cave and then a shadow darkened the cave wall and there he was, the ghost from her past, come back to haunt her. But it couldn't be. No, of course not. There are no such things as ghosts and you know it, Jenna.

He dumped the saddle-bags on the floor and rummaged in one. He had been to tend the horses and retrieve gear. He pulled out two squat yellowish tallow candle stumps and lit them with a match from his vest pocket. The flames didn't do much near the entrance, but as he walked back toward her, the lights gained in intensity until the cave filled with a warm glow that Jenna took small comfort in.

He stood by her feet and she finally looked up at him, sure that he wanted her to do so. But he wasn't looking at her. He was staring beyond her to the back of the cave, where the ceiling lowered and the darkness held fast. He stared at the pile of rocks, two feet tall and three times that long, just as Niall had promised her they'd left it.

The yellow light flickered in the chill

breeze from the open doorway, and still he stared at the grave. Finally he spoke, without looking at her.

'You know his name?'

'No,' she said.

'Well I do.' He turned to her, the candle held at face level, the sickly yellow light dancing in those dark eyes. 'He was my brother.'

He stared at her for a full minute. Relief and fear in equal measures washed over her. Finally she said, 'I'm sorry.' It wasn't true. She had no sorrow for him or his brother. What had been done was deserved.

He exhaled loudly and said, 'Not sorry enough. Yet.' He turned and walked to the front of the cave.

Now it made sense to her. Mad sense. He wanted revenge for his brother's death. But it was so long ago. Why now, after all these years? He should have, if not forgotten about it, at least tried to put it behind him and gotten on with his life. She knew that for some people forgetting, if not forgiving, was as impossible as climbing to the moon on a rope ladder.

If the past is never allowed to heal over, it's always a fresh wound. She could almost hear Drift saying something like that. This man had never allowed himself to heal. He kept his wound raw and ragged, poking it every day to remind himself of why he was alive, what he must do to live through each day.

She was the bait in a well-laid trap, that much was clear. He had taken great pains to mark their trail. Now she knew why. She sat stone-faced, staring into the near dark of the cold cave. He meant to lure Niall here. That damned range war had been Niall's fight then, though he had not wanted it, had not started it, and this man wanted to kill Niall to avenge his brother's death now.

Jenna breathed deeply. Though she still shivered with a cold that settled into the very marrow of her bones, she was grateful to be out of the wind and snow at last. If she told this man the truth of his brother's death, it would do nothing but remove any chance she might have of living through this. And Niall represented that chance. For she knew that Niall was looking for her even now, storm or no. She had been away from the ranch for more than a day and she had expected him, if he wasn't late, fully a half-day or more after she'd been taken from home. That meant that if nothing held him up he wouldn't have begun looking for her until dark last night, well after the storm began.

She hoped he didn't take one of his detours to check on his land on his way home from town. If ever there wasn't a time to explore it was now. But because of the storm, she doubted he would waste any time. If she knew Niall he would want to be back home safe and sound before the storm hit. They had a big head-start on him. But they were now done traveling. This cave was where this man intended to hole up and wait for Niall. Wait him out to kill him.

Uncle Drift would have followed if he could. But he was unconscious at best when they left him. It couldn't be good, or she would have heard from him by now. He felt as protective of her as any father might of his daughter.

That left Niall. And with a trail like that left by this madman, then it wouldn't be long before he showed up. She hoped. Unless the storm slowed him. Of course it would, she told herself. Think what you might about your husband, but he's only a man. Flesh and blood and no matter how tough he seems, he can't stop a bullet. And judging from the arsenal this man carried, two Colt pistols and two Winchester rifles, from what she saw, and plenty of ammunition, she guessed, in those heavy saddle-bags, he would be a formidable foe, especially from his superior vantage point in the cave that overlooked the only trail into the little canyon.

And then a thought occurred to her that seized her with the suddenness of a bullet. She had outlasted her usefulness to him. Now that he had her here, there was no other reason for him to keep her alive. He had fulfilled whatever logic he employed to uphold his end of the bargain. She was safely in the cave and Niall would know that he had taken her here from that blatant trail he left. Now it was just a matter of time before Niall showed up and this thing ended, one way or another. But would it end earlier than that for her?

What was stopping him from killing her now? Unless he wanted something more from her. She remembered eight years before, then she remembered his hand on her thigh that morning, and a chill passed through her. She looked up and saw him at the mouth of the cave.

'Didn't count on this storm. Bound to slow him down.'

The suddenness of his words woke her and she lifted her head from her chest. He was near the entrance to the cave, squatting and sipping coffee, both hands curled around a tin cup by the small fire he'd built just outside the cave opening. He stared into the thick weather, the snow storm raging just around the rocky cornice of the fire. He was well inside the cave, out of range of anybody who might aim for him.

'You seem to have thought of everything else,' she said.

He spun his head around and regarded her for a moment, as if he almost hadn't heard her. As if he had to think about what she said. He turned back to the fire and the swirling, howling entrance to the cave. Some minutes passed, then he spoke again, and again it was almost as if he were talking to himself. Jenna had to strain to hear him.

'Had a long time to think on it.'

16

It took Niall a healthy hour of riding, snaking in and out of trees, guessing where the trail lay before he found a tree with the slash mark he'd grown accustomed to seeing. It was right in line with what remained of Greasy's trail. Though the snow had long since covered Greasy's tracks, Niall guessed that Greasy had probably been on his own malnourished and ancient walnut mare. Niall had seen the poor beast at times in town, usually tied outside the saloon. Its hoofs were unshod and badly needed trimming, and the man's saddle was a sorry thing, dried out and curling with age and neglect. Now in addition to his own old horse, Greasy had the pony, too.

The wounds on the trees appeared with more frequency and Niall surveyed them closer from time to time.

And now that he did, he had to admit to himself that it was obvious they couldn't have been made by the gypsy man and his knife. The blade that made them was much larger, the bites it took were thick and deep, deeper at the top than at the bottoms. More downstrokes than up. Whoever it was had made them from horseback and from close up, the gypsy man couldn't have maneuvered the wagon tight enough to the trees to hack into them like that, even if his knife had been large enough to do such a job. Niall felt a brief twinge of shame for grabbing at his earlier conclusion, no matter the logic of it.

Snow caked in the wounds on the tree trunks. The frigid temperatures made it difficult for him to tell how long ago they had been hacked; the sap that normally wept from such a wound had not been able to weep due to the frigid temperatures.

He held Mackie back as they slid their way down an embankment, loose and shale-strewn under the snow. Niall kept his eyes on the ground under them, making sure Mackie didn't step wrong. With no warning the horse shied and reared. It was all Niall could do to hold the saddle until Mackie's forefeet came back down. The horse swung around parallel to the bank and Niall grabbed the moment to slip off, holding the reins hard and keeping the horse's head low so Mackie wouldn't rear again.

Between wrestling with the reins, the wind driving the snow in his face, and the horse punching up sodden sand and gravel, Niall couldn't make out what it was that spooked Mackie until they slid their way to the bottom of the bank. And then he saw it, a horse covered with snow and laid out right in their path.

Niall tied off Mackie to a tree well away from the beast, and he went over to take a look, expecting it to be one of the two of his horses unaccounted for. It wasn't Jenna's Sweet Baby and it wasn't his Slate. It was a thin, brown horse. And oddest of all, it was still alive. Niall brushed the snow from its face and body. He didn't see any wounds and no gear, just the markings on her face where a bridle had long rubbed. He bent low over the horse and heard a thin, rasping wheeze. The old horse was played out. He gazed at the big brown eye that barely blinked as snow fell on it, at the sunken flesh around the eyes, the emaciated temple and jaw. The body seemed to be sinking in on itself. He pulled off his mitten and patted the horse, stroking it under the chin, talking gently to her.

It was a testament to the horse it once was that she made it this far in this condition. And it was a damn shame, he thought, as he drew his pistol, that she had to end her days under the ownership of as vile a character as Greasy. He hesitated a moment, wondering if the shot would tip his hand to whoever had abducted Jenna. Then he thought of the hacked trees and knew they wanted him.

'I'm sorry, girl. Sleep now.' And he fired, sending the lead slug deep into the horse's brain. The body vibrated, the legs stiffened and held, then the big frame relaxed.

Mackie neighed and swung his head erratically, as if in disagreement in an argument. 'I'm sorry, boy,' said Niall. 'There was nothing to be done. She was gone already, her body just didn't know it yet.'

Niall stared down at what he had done and vowed that Greasy would pay individually and distinctly for each affront he had coming to him.

He closed the horse's staring eye and stroked her face once more, then led Mackie away from that place that already hosted the bitter tang of death. When they were up and over the other side of the gully, he remounted and resumed his search for slashed trees, not quite putting out of his mind the thing he just did, or the man who forced him to do it.

17

'Hey there in the cave!' Greasy thought it best to offer up a warning that he was here, especially considering the disposition of this fellow. Quiet sort and none too friendly, but then he had bought the drinks back in town.

Greasy slid down off the gypsy pony and yelled it again. He hoped the man was there and, what's more, he hoped he had some hot coffee and a little food for him. He hated being up here. It was creepy after all this time to be back in the jagged rocks, back at the cave. It had been eight years since the range war drove people all over these hills. He'd been deputized for the duration and had tried to make the best of it. He'd come out of it all right, considering. But he just couldn't get a fair shake since then and his fortunes had waned.

It wasn't true what everyone said about him that he was lazy, that he couldn't hold a job. He was just waiting for the right opportunities to come along instead of slaving away at things that just didn't make sense to him. And now it looked like a right thing was about to happen.

Greasy had his eyes fixed on the black cave opening. He must be in there. Why else would he ask all about it? Winters' place was empty, doors open, and that old fool Drift laid up in the barn with his head bleeding. Should have stayed there in the hay, holding his head. He was no help at all. The old fool just came at him all willy-nilly. Deserved what he got. Greasy continued to stare through the snow, up the slope at the maw of the cave and then the man was there, half his hat poking out of the dark, the front of his coat. Now Greasy could see thin smoke curling up by the entrance.

'Hey!' Greasy waved an arm, smiled up at the man.

He just stared down at Greasy for a few moments of silence, then said, 'What do you want?'

'You gonna find out,' said Greasy to himself, then he yelled, 'Now is that any way to greet a friend? I could use a cup of coffee.'

The man stared down at him, then waved him up to the cave with a hooked finger before turning inside.

'Well now that's more like it,' said Greasy, as he quickly looped the pony's reins over a broken branch. He scrambled up the slope, slipping to his knees twice, sliding backward and cursing. The snow was cold on his bare hands. He struggled to get upright and ended up crawling the last few feet to the flat space before the mouth of the cave.

He could sure use something warm in his belly. He bet this fellow had whiskey packed away, too. Greasy remembered the way the man had sipped his back in the bar. He hoped that didn't mean he was two steps away from being a teetotaler. At this point even coffee would be good. Then a bite of food, some money, and head on out of there. But he had to play it right or he might not take the bait. He'd come this far, there was no way he was going back empty-handed.

Greasy reached the snowy shelf and the man came out of the cave. 'What do you want?' He was definitely not too happy to see him. He stood with his hands on his waist, his coat pushed back over double pistols. The fire was small and just inside the cave, not far enough back to smoke them out unless the wind shifted, but the way the surrounding rock hung down it kept the wind in its place.

Greasy leaned forward, squinting through the snow and past the man's arm into the cave. There was a glow inside but not enough to see much of anything. 'You got anybody in there, friend? Like a certain little lady with a fiery temper?' He looked at the stranger.

'What do you want?' he said again, somewhere between a mumble and a growl.

'Well now.' Greasy straightened his back and made a show of smacking the snow from his pants and sleeves. 'I been thinkin' on what you told me about more money and all. And I been thinkin' not a little bit on why you were so all-fired curious to know just where Winters lived and where this God-forsaken hole in the rocks was located. And I come to the conclusion that you got something planned that's a little off. I figure we got an arrangement to make.' He folded his arms across his chest and just could not help but look at that man sort of sideways and with a bit of a smile. He had him right where he wanted him.

He still couldn't see the man's eyes but he heard him sigh. 'Get some coffee,' he motioned Greasy inside, 'and I'll tend to that pony of yours.'

Greasy rubbed his hands together. 'Now that's more like it, friend. Too darn cold out here to split hairs. And look, don't skimp on them oats. That little animal's got to get me back to town. After I eat, that is.' He giggled and ducked into the cave.

It took a bit to get used to the near-black of the cave. He crouched low over the little fire, warming his hands, and tossed a couple of pieces of wood on after stirring it up a bit. Smoke rose up in his face and he coughed and spat. The chipped coffee pot was warm. He poured himself a cup and scanned the depths of the cave. Back there, a candle burned with a paltry flame on a rock shelf. He walked to it, sipping his coffee and curling his numb fingers around the warm cup. He heard a scuffing sound at his feet and thought of snakes or a hibernating animal. He jumped back, then leaned forward. 'Who's there?'

'Greasy? Is that you?' a woman's voice whispered.

He leaned closer and said, 'Mrs Winters?'

'Yes, Greasy. Oh thank God. Help me before he comes back. Quick, my feet and hands are tied.' He heard her scuff the sandy cave floor.

He raised his eyebrows. 'That a fact?'

'Greasy, hurry. With your help we might take him by surprise and get out of here.'

He bent down, felt for her feet. His breathing was faster now. He felt the tip of her boots, worked a hand up the boot to the rope, knotted tight around her ankles. And he swallowed and could not help himself. It was like the half-finished glasses of beer still on the tables in the saloon at night when he swept up. They just sat there, foam gone, wiggling as he jostled the table. His hand slid up past the rope, touched not bare skin as he expected but long underwear and it did not matter.

'Greasy!' she whispered. 'What are you doing? Untie my feet. Help me quick!'

He licked his lips and grunted. His mind moved fast. This woman was bound to die, if Greasy had read the stranger right. So what would it matter? He would never get this chance again. His hand slid higher up her leg, above her knee and at the same time he grabbed at her chest, hooked a finger behind the collar at her throat and yanked. Buttons popped off, hitting him in the face. He grunted again.

'No!' she shouted, too loud, and kicked him square in the chest with both booted feet. His breath left him and he collapsed on top of her, gasping. She beat him on the head, swinging her bound hands down on him like a club and working her knees to get him off of her. And then he felt himself sliding backward.

His hand came out from under the warmth of her dress where it had been trapped. He felt something grab the back of his pants and lift him up. When he swung around, it was just light enough in the cave to see one side of the stranger before a fist drove into Greasy's face. He let him go then and

215

Greasy slapped into the rock wall, his back first and then his head bounced off a pointed nub of rock.

'Hey!' he managed to get out, before a fist pushed into his stomach. It felt as if it touched his spine. He fell to his knees, clutching at his gut and retching. He threw up the turkey he had taken from the gypsy wagon and hung over the little puddle, strings of saliva connecting him to it. He looked up just as the man grabbed for him again. Greasy had barely enough time to tense, but the man didn't hit him again.

Instead he clawed at Greasy's belt, ripped apart his buttons and pulled down on his pants. 'Hey,' said Greasy again, but it didn't matter. The man was stripping him down. Every time Greasy fought him the man slapped his face hard, back and forth, and then resumed stripping him. He ripped Greasy's clothes off. Greasy heard a soft tearing sound and his shirt whipped off. Before he could shiver he was flipped face first into the dirt and held upside down by the boots. The man shook him out of his boots and then he was fully naked.

He curled up on the floor and pushed himself against the far wall. The man threw Greasy's boots and in two steps he was standing above Greasy. He kicked him in the ribs, the arms, the legs, the head, over and over. Throughout the beating the stranger never made a sound.

Greasy heard someone shouting and he knew it wasn't himself because he couldn't even catch his own breath.

'Stop it! Stop it! You're killing him! Stop it!' Over and over it seemed he heard this. And finally he recognized it as Mrs Winters' voice. And then the kicking stopped. He was close to blacking out and he tried to curl up but he couldn't pull his legs up enough. He throbbed all over.

The man picked him up by the hair. It didn't even hurt, but Greasy slapped at him just the same. Through his one eye that could still open, he saw the man point with his other hand at the shouting woman. The man didn't say a thing, just pointed. She stopped yelling.

Then he turned and dragged Greasy toward the front of the cave. 'What? What are you doing?' But Greasy's words sounded like mush. Without hesitation the man dragged him right outside and bending down, grabbed one of Greasy's ankles.

'My pony,' Greasy whimpered. 'Lemme have my pony.'

The man paused. For the first time that day Greasy could see his eyes. They looked right at him and he just shook his head. Then he swung Greasy back toward the cave, then forward and let go of him. He pitched Greasy into the air over the rocks that led up to the cave. Greasy managed a scream but it was cut off as he landed face first on the rocks near the base of the slope.

How long he lay there he didn't know. After some time he was aware of snapping sounds all around him. He was beginning to feel the cold and then something stung him. And again. He looked up and the sounds grew louder. He saw the hazy shape of someone way up there pointing in his direction. Then he heard that noise. It sounded like shooting.

He opened his eyes wide and looked again. The stranger was shooting at him. Greasy pushed himself up to his hands and knees. He did not feel so good. He could hear his ragged breaths and he could only see out of one eye. He had many broken bones, he was sure of it. As he swayed there in the snow he began to shake and within moments his entire body quivered from the cold.

Another shot sounded and he felt the stinging again. It was rock chips pelting him from the bullets. 'Go,' said a voice. It was the stranger. He couldn't be serious. Where was he to go? He had no clothes and his pony was nowhere to be seen. Probably ran off, he thought. Then he remembered the look the man had given him when he'd asked about the pony. Another shot sounded and he felt a punch in his lower leg. He looked down and a chunk was missing from the back of his leg. He felt no pain, he guessed he was too cold for that. He screamed but it came out ragged and was too much work. He stopped, choking and trying to swear.

'Go.'

Another shot sounded and Greasy watched his left hand explode inches under his face. This time he screamed loud and long and when he ran out of breath he heard that voice above him say, 'Go.'

He dragged himself down the rest of the rocks to the flat trail-like section at the bottom. It was still snowing and the wind was bitter and slicing. He knew he would die and half-thought of just lying down and letting the man plug away at him until it was all over. But something long buried, the barest shadow of pride in the man he used to be, kept him dragging forward. He thought of his mother, 'You never know,' echoing in his head. But she was wrong, because there comes a time when you do know. You know everything you ever will know.

He used his knees and his one good hand to drag himself back the way he came a short while before. As he heaved and sobbed his way down the ragged mountain, the red smear he left trailing behind him in the snow was covered in minutes with a pristine white layer.

18

A shift in the wind squalled snow in Niall's face. He pulled up on Mackie's reins and waited for it to pass. A faint sound came to him from the north-east like stones hitting others below the surface of water. Was it trees protesting under the weight of so much sudden heavy snow? The ice storm of four winters back had flattened a number of trees, snapped the tops off others. Despite the intervening seasons, the results would be evident for years yet. Had it been gunshots? From the north-east? There was no defined trail except the one he'd been forced to follow this far — the slashed trunks were frequent enough that he was confident of his direction. But those sounds . . . if they were gunshots and they were from the north-east . . . His destination occurred to him wholly formed. He knew where he must go.

The only place of relevance north-east of his current location had been the cave. That vile cave. He thought he'd seen the last of it, but now he knew for sure that he would see it again. Maybe one last time. But why the cave? Surely it would be an appropriate place to hole up during a storm, but only if someone happened to be that far up in the mountains. And only if someone knew of its where-abouts. It was situated so that unless you were practically on top of it even an experienced man of the mountains might not find the opening. Could he be wrong? It could well be that the direction of the shots was just coinci-dence. Or a trick of the wind. But the continued north-easterly track of the slashed trees bore out his thinking.

He nudged Mackie and from then on Niall let memory guide him. To his satisfaction, they were led right by the slash marks he had been following. There was no trail, hadn't been since the slashes departed from the old road about where he met up with the gypsies. Their speed was hampered by the sheer amount of snow that fell in the past day. But the trees, mostly aspen and spruce, grew sparse enough that in places three riders abreast could make their way up the rising landscape.

As Niall rode, letting Mackie choose his footing, urging the horse forward when the sometimes chest-high snow threatened to strand them, he pressed the horse on toward the cave. Though it had been eight years, Niall remembered precisely where it was, and he also knew that whoever was there first would have the advantage over whoever was next to ride up the only entrance to the little canyon.

He reasoned that his best chance for maintaining an element of surprise was to cut south and circle behind the cave's peak, what was it called? Preble Tip? Something like that. Since the range war he had not once visited this section of his land and he could see no reason to change his mind after this. If there was to be an after. He shook away the thought and looked upward through the trees. It was well past midday, though it was mostly his stomach that told him so. He half-regretted giving so much of his food to the gypsies but there was a good chance that he wouldn't need food all that much longer. There was also the chance that they wouldn't either.

The snow rose in the gullies and each step took a toll on Mackie. Niall lowered himself out of the saddle and into waist-deep snow. Back a bit, a stand of aspens and scrubbier under-growth offered a relatively sheltered respite from the wind. Here the snow reached Mackie's knees but no higher. Niall tied off the horse, fed him, gave him the last of the water from the canteen, and unloaded his blankets and saddle-bags. He strapped on the snow-shoes and tramped down the area surrounding Mackie.

'It'll have to do for now, my friend.' Niall ate the last half of a hard biscuit, scooped a small handful of snow and chewed it down while his face was uncovered, then filled his pockets with the rest of the loose ammunition from his saddle-bags, wrapped his face well with an oversize kerchief, pulled on his fur mittens, and pulled down his fur hat. He was as ready as he would ever be. He patted Mackie's rump and said, 'I'll be back. Bet on it,' though he said it more for his own benefit than Mackie's. The wind whipped the words away as soon as he said them. The horse stood hunched and facing with the wind, his ears down.

Once Niall stepped out of the scant thicket, a blast caused a momentary whiteout in front of him. He stood still, braced against it, then continued on as the gust abated. He figured it would be another couple of miles until the little craggy peak came into view. As he remembered, there was little around it and the land opened up before it, affording whoever was holed up there a fine view of all comings and goings below and into the little canyon. But not behind it.

He would get as close as he dared, then venture over the ridge, climbing up behind the peak from the south. The landscape was compact at that range. It shouldn't take him long. And he could move with more ease the closer he got to the peak as the snow would not be nearly as deep out on the windswept and bare rocky spot.

Once he got there it was anybody's guess as to who he would find and what might happen. He gritted his teeth and swore for the thousandth time that day that if he found Jenna in any state other than her normal self, there would be no quarter given by him.

He trudged on, squinting through the slowing snow. The wind, too, was losing its gumption. He heard a groan at the same time his right snowshoe slipped off something spongy. He lost his balance and flopped sideways into the snow. He kept his rifle raised above the snow and twisted onto his back, scrambling backward away from whatever it was that groaned.

Through the hide webbing of his snowshoes he saw what looked like bare skin in the scuffed snow — and something else that caused his heart to catch and claw in his throat. He dropped the rifle and grabbed at the thing, keeping his snowshoes well clear of it. It was a person. And there beneath his frantic, pawing mittens were the bold knitted reds and greens of Jenna's house shawl. She always wore it about the place for most of three seasons and even on the cooler summer nights. He teased her about it, that it had more repairs than the barn roof, but still she kept it (though never wearing it when they had visitors, he often pointed out with a wink).

And now here it was and as he pawed away the snow from this naked body, he was shocked and relieved all at once. Shocked to see the bare skin beneath him was marbled and splotched bright red and brilliant blue. And relieved to find that it was not Jenna near dead in the snow. It was someone who had received a severe beating, judging from the swollen face.

Niall lifted the head and torso into his lap and he realized it was Greasy. The town bum. And molester of gypsies and a possible killer and kidnapper. But if he was the guilty man whom he had been tracking, then who had given him such a severe beating? It would not be Jenna, even when pressed she could not do such a thing.

He bent low over the swollen and almost unrecognizable face and said, 'Greasy! Where is my wife? Greasy, it's Niall Winters. Where is my wife?' There was no response. Though Niall detected no breath from the man's ragged mouth, the man was still alive, his chest showing the slightest of movements.

'Greasy! Answer me!' Niall shouted now, shaking the battered man. 'Where did you get her shawl? Greasy, where is Jenna?'

The man opened a slitted, reptile-like eye. They eyeball roved left and right, unable to focus. 'Winters? That you?' The voice came in a hoarse, muted whisper.

'Yes, Greasy. It's me. It's Niall Winters. Where's my wife?'

The abused man smiled and tried to speak. He coughed and a wash of pain further blanched his distorted features. He swallowed with effort and said, 'He come at me . . . the fork. Gypsies don't got no gold.'

So Greasy had killed Uncle Drift. It was all Niall could do to keep from twisting off the man's head right then and there. 'Where's my wife? Where's Jenna Winters, Greasy? Have you seen her?' Niall slapped the man on the face. Greasy closed his eye and swallowed again. 'Cave's a bad place . . . bad luck.'

'Is she at the cave, Greasy? Is my wife at that cave? Is somebody with her?' But Greasy didn't respond. His breaths were less frequent and more labored.

'Winters.' It was a cold sound, barely a whisper.

Niall heard it. 'What?'

'Name's not Greasy.' He stopped, swallowed, and tried to lick his lips. He opened his eye and tried to focus. 'Joe Tanner. Always been.'

Niall looked down on him with no pity. 'This world's a hard enough place without people like you in it, Joe Tanner. Good riddance.'

The beaten man's features contorted as if he just heard terrible news and Niall saw the naked chest rise, hold, then sink back down and relax and rise no more. He stared at him a moment, then got up. He pulled Jenna's shawl from beneath the dead man, shook it once and stuffed it inside his coat. He grabbed in the snow until he found his rifle, then he headed up the ridge to the south of the cave.

19

'Why did you — ?'

But he cut her off. 'I spent seven years surrounded by men like that. And I won't be second to any such a man.'

It took her a few moments to comprehend what he meant. She pushed herself backward with her feet, pulling her dress together at the top where Greasy had ripped it apart. She squirmed, wriggled close to the cave wall.

'I went in there I was a young man. Young in every way.' He pointed down at her. 'I was robbed by your husband.'

'I . . . I don't understand. Niall hasn't done anything to you. He doesn't know you.'

He sighed and stared at his brother's grave. 'I was just a kid when my brother went off on a job. Hired himself out as a gun hand to help with a range war.

Chose the wrong side, got himself killed.'

He turned back to her, staring at her face, his hat pulled low. 'He raised me. Then he never come back. Said that was gonna be the last time he left. Gonna make enough to buy us some land, have our own place.' He snorted and said, 'An' I believed him,' shaking his head.

Jenna wanted to ask why he thought Niall was responsible for robbing him but she didn't dare open her mouth. She had seen his anger at work and had no desire to be on the receiving end of it.

'Took to stealing to stay alive. But I was dumb. Got caught. I was a big kid, they didn't believe I was only fourteen. Put me in Yuma and forgot about me for seven years.'

He walked to the front of the cave and stared out into the snow. So that was it. Straight-out revenge.

He hadn't tried anything yet, so Jenna worked to tie her dress back

233

together before he looked at her again. Her hands shook, a mixture of the increasing cold and fear. She didn't want to draw any attention to herself. If she could just hold on until Niall came. She knew he would come for her. He could track a ram over rocky terrain. Uncle Drift had bragged on Niall's tracking abilities so often she'd take for granted that he was one of the best around. And even if he wasn't, it wouldn't matter. The trail this stranger left was blatant enough.

He would be here, she was sure of it. Unless something happened to him. No, she wouldn't allow herself to think like that. She was letting her thoughts run and they weren't heading in a useful direction. She concentrated on picturing Niall finding their location.

The stranger walked back toward her, the other candle in his hand, and looked down at her, the flames reflecting and dancing in his eyes. She didn't like what she saw on his face and she thought desperately for something to say, blurting the first thing she thought of to distract him. 'What did you steal to keep you in prison for seven years?'

He looked at her for a moment, then half smiled, the first she saw crack his stony features. But the cold smile told her that he knew why she asked.

He rubbed a dirty hand on his stubbled mouth, wiping away the smile, and said, 'A donkey. To sell so I could buy food. But what you really wanna know is how I came to know where my brother was laid to rest. Am I right?'

She stared at him, then nodded.

'Reckon we got plenty of time.' He sat down across from her, leaning against the cave wall, his legs drawn up, and he sighed. He looked as close to a kid then as he ever would, she decided. He pulled a pistol and rested it in his lap.

Over his knees he stared at her and said, 'A guard told me. He was a braggart. Told me plenty. Used to be a deputy. Helped with the clean up after your husband killed everybody in his damn range war.'

Jenna clenched her jaw tight to keep from shouting down the comment. She was here during the war; this fool wasn't.

'Told me by the time they got up here, wasn't much they could do but cover him with rocks.' He spat the words as if they were rancid and he turned to face the rock pile at the rear of the cave. He was quiet for a time. Jenna didn't move. She looked down at her hands, waiting to hear if he would resume. He did.

'I got plenty of information from him over a few years. 'Til somebody killed him.' He looked back at her. 'But not before I got enough to get me here.'

⋆　⋆　⋆

Jenna knew that if Niall stood a chance at all of making it to the cave he would have to come straight in from the front, the same way they had come into the narrow canyon with the cave at its head. It was the only way in. She had to keep this man talking, keep him from spending all his time at the mouth of the cave watching for Niall.

Given the great pains he took to mark a trail for Niall to follow, she didn't think he would shoot at her husband until he had the chance to explain to Niall his twisted motives for doing this. But he obviously also did not want to be caught unawares. If she learned anything about this madman it was that he did nothing without giving it careful consideration. And he also needed to maintain an edge of control at all times. He did not like to have control of a situation taken from him.

Maybe that's the key, she thought. Maybe I need to keep him just angry enough to argue with me and then he'll forget the entrance. And maybe that will give Niall enough time to make his way in. That's a wagonload of maybes, Jenna old girl, she told herself. But it's the best I can do. She tested the bonds on her wrists and ankles once again.

He walked back from the cave entrance and stared down at her again. She didn't like it. She'd seen that look too many times before from the time she could drive a trap into town on her own and it wasn't a friendly look.

'Look, you don't even know the first thing about the fight that took place here because of this land. All you know is what you choose to believe and what other people have told you and that's all third-hand news. I was here: I know what happened. And if you're going to go around killing people for something that you had no place in then the least you can do is hear the truth of it.'

Jenna felt the heat rise in her face and her heart raced. She was talking back to this young killer and she didn't care. He had better listen. He just stared at her, no reaction at all. Just like a stone statue.

She swallowed and continued, 'Niall was here for years before that thief, Père Boudleaux — his band of yes-men called him Père — came in one day on the stage, waving some paper around that he says put him in claim of a thousand acres, most of which was Niall's land.'

'But Niall had that land locked up tight and legal. He and Drift bought it a couple of years before that. That was about a year before I knew him. They worked hard to carve the place out of nothing and Boudleaux offered well below what the land was worth, not that Niall would ever sell anyway, let alone take him seriously. Boudleaux just wanted the land for logging — it's the timber on this land that makes it so valuable. He claimed his offer was a gift. Said that he didn't even have to offer any money at all because he was the rightful owner of the land. But his claim, all his papers, were all false. And the sad thing is, everybody knew it. But no one would stand up to him except Niall and Drift and a few of their friends, like the Dibbses and the sheriff. But the sheriff was one of the first people killed, by the way, and he was a dear friend to Niall and Uncle Drift.'

Jenna looked across at the kid. He was watching her. Good, she thought. The longer and more interesting I can make this story, the better chance I can give Niall to get up the canyon without being seen.

Jenna continued, 'Niall sent to Cheyenne for a federal marshal and a lawyer, but before they could get here Boudleaux made his big push, figured if he killed us off, no one would dare put up a fight for the land. And he was probably right, considering that so few people challenged him up to that point. He brought in a pile of hired guns, some we later heard, came from as far away as Arizona and Texas, all to participate in what he called a 'just action'. But it was just murder, plain and simple. A gang of murderers and thieves looking to make easy money.'

She looked right at him then and tried to keep from saying it, but she couldn't help herself. 'And your brother was a part of it.' Jenna knew she had gone beyond trying to keep him from going to the cave's entrance.

He stretched his legs out, one hand still on the pistol, and said, 'Maybe what you're saying is true, maybe it ain't. Truth be told it don't matter none to me because I figure you were all in on it, kickin' up that range war of yours, and so you're all as guilty as the next person. All this talk ain't gonna give me my seven years back, now is it?' He stood up.

'So your answer is to blame everyone? With your logic then the sort of revenge you seek would never come to an end. According to your way of thinking, the sheriff would be guilty for not stopping Boudleaux when he first came into town on that stage, waving his false land-grant claim, even though Niall had his deed assayed and registered in Cheyenne years before.

'And then the men who hired on to drive Niall and Drift off the land by any means necessary would all be hunted

241

down and killed. Because as sure as it's snowing and blowing right now they helped instigate the range war. And by now many of those men have probably grown weary and settled down, had wives and children of their own. They, too, every last woman and child, should be killed because they most surely would know of the range war.

'And the saloon keepers, that would be the Waites, Cornell and Eunice, and their son, Jasper, who was working in the saloon at the time — he's now a bank president, by the way, in Aldarta, and they're proud of him — they all waited on the men who fought in the range war, including your brother, I've no doubt. And then of course there's the stage operator, he brought the people in, and the federal marshal and the lawyer, who came all the way from Cheyenne. And because it was such a mess there was a governor at the time who signed a proclamation — let's see, where is he now . . . ' She scrunched her face up, scanning the air as if the answer was written somewhere on the cave wall. 'Oh yes, I believe he resides back East now, in a place called Washington. Rumor has it he has designs on being President.'

'Shut your mouth, woman.' She had no warning as he lashed out. The back of his knuckle-scarred hand caught her full on the mouth. The fact that he hit her was far worse than the throbbing and the blood she felt trickle from her split lower lip. Far worse was the memory the knuckled hand brought to mind. No one had hit her in eight years. Not since this man's older brother had hit her in the same manner, the same knuckled backhand, the same split lip. And in the same cave. She never thought she would relive this.

He walked away toward the front of the cave and stirred life into the faint fire, then walked outside to once again scan the little valley. Maybe she made things worse by angering him, she thought. Maybe now he'll shoot Niall as soon as he sees him.

She closed her eyes and rested her head forward, her chin nearly touching her chest. She made a sound like a dog as it runs in its dreams. She made it again and laughed, louder now, knowing she could not control herself. She thought the man had hit her, just as his brother had, because they were both raised by an abusive man whose wife put up with his abuse. They might have grown up thinking that hitting a woman was not such a bad thing, or perhaps they themselves felt the oppressive hand of an abusive parent.

She thought that if she and Niall ever had kids they would have raised them to know that there are better ways of settling a problem than with violence. But she didn't think that anything other than violence would solve the problem they now faced. And she didn't know if even that would save them this time. It was in the midst of such a thought that Jenna dozed off, exhausted and emotionally drained, into a fitful sleep.

20

The snow stopped and a subtle breeze glazed the surface of the heavy snowpack. Niall took in a deep breath through his nostrils and let it out slowly. Wood smoke. He must be conscious of every sound he might make until he gained entrance to the cave. If he got that far. He trudged forward. And within seconds the gray nub came into view, rising with each labored step he made with the snow-shoes. Instead of feeling pleased at finally seeing his goal, he realized he was just dog-tired. He worked on the ragged edge of exhaustion. Every step fought him and every breath pushed and pulled from him as though he were losing an argument with a cross-cut saw.

He looked up through the spiked tree-line at the back of the little peak.

Below him the land sloped at a manageable angle for a few hundred yards, then beyond that the slope was severe, and beyond that, a cliff gave way to a long drop hundreds of feet down with a sudden and rocky stop at the bottom. Losing his balance and toppling backward was not a possibility.

He held his breath and leaned into the hill, grabbing at the talus slope, the shale-covered surface visible only in patches where snow found it difficult to adhere. He slid back half a step for each step forward. Once he gained purchase at the base of the peak he would have to shed the snowshoes. They would be too cumbersome to allow him to make the final push to the peak.

As he climbed, he thought again about the prudence of approaching the cave from the rear. There was no other direction from which he might gain the element of surprise on the kidnapper. The man had marked his trail like someone who fully expected to be followed, indeed, never was an intention clearer to Niall, but that didn't mean Niall had to saunter on up the one trail that led into the little canyon, at the head of which sat the cave, poised like a staring snake. Niall did not relish the thought of laying himself open to such a snakebite.

Tricky as the climb would be, the element of surprise was his best bet. He'd been in enough dicey situations in the past to know that the sliver of chance that it would give him just might mean the difference between living and dying. He was also all too aware that the more time he spent crawling through snow was time not spent freeing Jenna.

He reached the first of several mansize spears of rock sticking up like ragged teeth. He maneuvered around to the uphill side of it and leaned there, catching his breath. There seemed to be no place he could duck out of the wind. He worked on shedding his snowshoes. The knots on the rawhide strapping were crusted thick with frozen snow and his mittens were useless on them. He pulled them off with his teeth, cradling the rifle tight in the crook of his arm.

As he scratched at the knots a gust swept granular snow into his face from the top of the peak. He flinched and closed his eyes and his mittens slipped from his mouth. He grabbed for them but the wind carried them, sliding and skittering across the smooth surface, until they disappeared over the first drop forty feet below him. 'Stupid!' he growled through his gritted teeth. He adjusted his grip on the rifle, determined not to let go of it, and succeeded in slipping the snowshoe straps off his boot heels. He tugged the snowshoes the rest of the way off and wedged them into the snow against the rock, hoping he'd be able to get back for them.

He entered the crevice that separated the cave's peak from the base of its much larger sibling to the north-east. It was packed below with drifted snow and the sides were slick with ice. From where he had stopped a few minutes before on the slope to get an idea of how he could approach the peak, he couldn't see these difficulties. And now here he was, just a few hundred feet from the entrance to the cave with no visible way forward. Has to be a way, he thought. He tested the drifted snow and found that though he sank nearly a foot, the snow beneath was packed dense enough that it supported him if he didn't make sudden moves.

He stretched both arms and found he could grab with his hands at the stone. He inched himself upward in this manner enough to do the same with his feet. He wedged a boot on either side of the crevice and moved forward at the same time. Progress was slow because he had his rifle encircled by the thumb and forefinger of his left hand, using the rest of his fingers to grip and push against the icy rock wall. The rifle clunked with each shuffling move. He cursed himself for not rigging a shoulder strap for the weapon.

His bare hands stiffened and ached. He kept his gaze fixed on several random stubs of rock that might afford a hand- or foothold, if he could just reach them. He looked down between his legs and was surprised to see the snow pack already a dozen feet below. He alternated each arm and leg, brought the left arm forward and skinned his knuckles along the porous rock. He couldn't pull his hand away or all his progress would be lost. Bright red blood welled on his knuckles, then streamed down his hand, disappearing beneath his coat cuff. He felt a warm tickle run down his arm and stop when it hit some fold in his clothing. More blood dripped off his fingertips and onto the ice-slick rock wall.

His hand and arms trembled and he knew if he didn't reach the aid of those rocks, still a good five feet ahead, he would drop into the crevice and have to crawl his way out and begin again. That is if he didn't break a leg down on a jagged mess of rock hidden beneath the snow. He made a choice then that he didn't want to have to make, but there was no other way. He parted his fingers and let the Winchester skid and slide down the stone face and wedge down there, pointing up at him from the deep snow.

Niall had made enough progress that he figured he was at approximately the same depth as the back of the cave. How thick the stone walls and ceiling were he did not know. He tried to remember back to his brief visit here eight years before, but it was no use. He had concentrated on Drift and on his future wife that day and not on the geographic features of the place, though he doubted that any of the noises he was capable of making out here would make their way through the rock.

By the time he reached the projecting stubs of rock he was exhausted. His limbs trembled and he felt with each shuffling move forward that he might collapse into the chasm, now forty feet or more below his quivering legs. The first nub was enough for him to grip and push on. He prayed it was not crumbly rock. It held. He leaned more of his weight on it and pushed off the right-side wall of the chasm, pivoting his body and grabbing at the next rock three feet up the wall from the first.

His fingers locked onto it and his body slammed into the rock wall and the weight of his body pulled his hand free from it. He hung there by his left hand, blood running down it freely, his right arm waving at nothing. He skittered back and forth like a clock pendulum, working the toes of his boots against the iced rock surface, getting closer to the rock with each swing. He grabbed it, missed, swung and grabbed at it again.

His fingertips found purchase. He was thankful there was no ice on the projecting stone, but he could feel the skin scraping off the fingertips of both hands. He pulled up on the right hand and readjusted the fingers of his left hand, regaining his grip. He hung like that for half a minute, his eyes closed, his breath coming in gasps, his raw cheek flush against the side of the cliff.

Now, he thought, looking up. All I have to do is pull myself up until my feet are where my hands are now. Simple. He closed his eyes and swallowed again, gaining control of his breathing. He willed his power upward and prayed that all those years of physical labor cutting trees, mucking stalls, building barns, fences, and houses would pay off for this very moment. His muscles, beyond burning, were jagged wires of glowing metal pain.

He scrabbled with the toes of his boots, grabbing rock when he could, slipping on the icy surface and then he was up. His hands now at waist level, he managed to raise one knee up on a nub, pulled his hand out, and grabbed one of many handholds above. He was nearly to the top of the peak now. He swung his other hand upward but it didn't come into view.

He looked down and saw he was kneeling on his own fingertips. They were so cold he couldn't feel them. He shifted his weight and swung the hand upward, hoping he could still grip. He stood. He rushed a couple of deep breaths. He didn't trust that his hands would work for much longer and he would rather get to the relative safety of the top of the peak than risk blowing on his hands here on the rock's face.

One more pull upward and he gained the top. Then it was a matter of low-crawling across the lopsided little peak until he was near the entrance. From that point he could either drop down, or if it was too far to drop, then find a side route down either side of the cave entrance, keeping a weapon drawn the entire time.

But first he must warm his hands. There was no way he could pull a trigger, let alone hold a pistol, just yet. He fumbled with his coat buttons, leaning against a lichen covered boulder, and after a minute of struggle thrust his hands tight under his arms. He crouched there, his face bleeding, his hands bleeding, and looked toward the front of the peak where he guessed anywhere from ten to twenty feet below lay the top of the cave entrance.

Niall alternated between blowing on his cupped hands and wiggling them under his arms and within a few minutes he had a bit of feeling back in them. He knew they would be sore but he also knew that unless he got moving he wouldn't care much one way or the other. Jenna, hang on, he muttered. I'm coming.

He low-walked toward where he hoped the cave would be, rubbing his hands together as he felt his way over the craggy knob. He stopped a good twenty feet before the edge of the peak and saw the land slope away forty feet down. The cave entrance was just below. He recognized the snow-daubed boulders, one twice as tall as a man and twenty feet around, halved by a mighty lightning strike who knows how long ago. It lay split like a massive egg, marking the flat, foyer-like entrance to the cave.

He suspected the peak over the cave entrance sloped backward to somewhere about where his feet now stood, though the rock seemingly continued another fifteen feet from his boots to the edge. But it was just a projecting shelf of drifted snow, apt to separate and drop off with little urging. He didn't dare advance further toward the shelf. He looked to his right to where the chasm he had scaled ended in a pinch fifteen feet or so before the little flat area before the cave.

No easy way down. No easy way to sneak down without being seen. A slight breeze carried wood smoke upward toward him. He had first smelled this fire an hour ago. Long enough, Winters. Time to move. No easy way down, so I'll make one.

He split the two handfuls of bullets between his two outer coat pockets, folding the flaps in for easy access. He drew both pistols, checked his chambers, and crouching, walked as far to the right as he could go. The rock sloped for a few yards, then dropped away and he knew once he started sliding down there was no stopping himself until he was deposited at the bottom, probably thirty feet from where he would start. He inhaled deeply and said in a low voice, 'I'm coming, Jenna.'

And he stepped off and down the chutelike drop.

* * *

Drifted chunks of snow flopped downward all around him. He kept his pistols out in front of him and raised, out of harm's way. Halfway down his right leg fetched up on a projecting tooth of rock. He hung up there for a moment, pulling his leg, ignoring the pain. It didn't feel broken. Good. He didn't need that to slow him down. He watched and gritted his teeth as hunks of stiff, drifted snow toppled out of the crevice before him and splayed out over the little plateau. Well, he thought. If that didn't tip them off then what would?

Niall waited fifteen feet up, tucked in the front edge of the crevice. He pulled his right leg free. All he had to do was step off again and slide the rest of the way down. Plenty of snow now, he thought. This was not going as he had planned. Not at all. The only hope he had now was that whoever was inside that cave would think the sun might have worked on the drifted snow enough to topple the snow shelf.

Niall pulled back when he heard a scuffing sound, then saw the tip of a black boot send a headsize chunk of snow bounce off others before flying off to the right where footsteps led away and down into the packed snow. If Niall remembered correctly, that was another gouge in the rock near the trail below that made a decent place to keep horses corralled.

The crunching footsteps receded,

stopped, then grew louder again. A tall man with long hair under a dirty black hat, black overcoat, and dirty brown woolen pants and knee boots strode by, looking down the slope as he went. The steps faded. Tending his horses? If he's alone then that is the man. And that means Jenna's in the cave. He pushed himself down the last of the snow slide and landed upright, grunting as he put weight on his jammed leg for the first time and finding it near useless, the pain shooting up from his heel in a hot surge. More snow chunks thumped and clunked all around him.

He held his pistols out, poised in opposite directions, and looked to his right first, covering the sloping path to the horses, hoping the man was out of sight. Then a quick glance to the left, and there was the cave entrance not ten feet away. No one came back up the path at him. He looked back to the cave and hobbled backward, keeping to the rock wall. Snow fell down his coat, chilling him.

For the time it took his breath to leave his mouth, the vapor rising in front of his face, a grim thought passed through his mind that made him fear entering the cave. What would he find? The only person in the world he loved left alive and what if . . . ? Less than a heartbeat later he pushed into the cave, hugging the wall and hoping for a miracle.

21

He shambled away from the cave entrance into the dark to his right. It wouldn't do to be silhouetted against the light of the outdoors if there were others inside, though they would surely have seen him by now. The entrance lay to his left with the smoldering campfire at his feet.

'Jenna!' he whispered into the dark. A brief dragging sound made him pause. Someone or something was back there. 'Jenna!' he hissed again, squinting into the dark.

'Niall? Niall, is it you?'

It was Jenna's voice, cracked and weary, but it was his Jenna. Never, he thought, in the history of the world has a man felt such relief. 'Yes! Are you all right?'

'Yes, I'm not hurt but I'm tied — '

'How many are there?'

'Just one. He must be checking the horses. Niall, I want to see you.'

'No! I want to keep him up here, away from you.'

'He's brutal. He beat Greasy pretty bad.'

'I know.'

'But — '

A third voice, that of a man younger than Niall's thirty-eight years, though deeper, crackled through their whispered exchange.

'You come over the top.'

Niall's instinct forced him into a low crouch, both pistols trained on the entrance. The man made a statement, nothing more. He could have been remarking on the amount of snow they'd received. Niall did not reply.

'Didn't think it was passable.'

Niall waited a few moments, then said, 'It's not.'

He heard a grunt in acknowledgement. Niall eased down onto his left knee and waited. His right leg throbbed. He had no idea what might happen next but by answering the man, Niall confirmed what the man already knew, probably because of Niall's boot prints in the snow, that Niall was in the cave.

He heard a rustling noise at the rear of the cave. He wanted to tell Jenna to keep still but he didn't want the man to locate him. Niall had the upper hand in the situation, a paltry one at best, but it was something anyway. And this man knew it.

From where Niall waited, he saw out and around the side of the entrance. The man was beyond this, though not far from the entrance for his voice to carry as it did without shouting.

'You got lucky, Winters. It won't happen twice.'

A crunching sound accompanied the last word and Niall knew the man was on the move. He tensed and said, 'Jenna, get down!'

The stranger came in low and fast, his two pistols flashing fire in the dim cavern. The echoes, with the snapping and pinging of ricocheting bullets, fought for escape. Niall's guns matched him note for note and the flash from his pistols killed any advantage the dark may have given him. The stranger, he saw, was no stranger to close-range fighting. He kept low and stuck to the dark for concealment. The stale, cold air of the cave was filled with the smell of gunpowder and thick smoke. Niall wanted to cough, to rinse his eyes with cool water.

He felt a trickle of warmth down his face and wondered if he'd been hit. The stranger had made it well into the cave. Niall saw a dim shape crouched ten feet in against the wall. They both fired another volley at the same time and, as Niall dove toward the back of the cave, he felt the unmistakable sting of a bullet in his upper arm. The shot caught him off guard and he stumbled, a boot snagging on a fragment of rock. He pitched forward and flipped into the wall, landed wrong, and pushed off the rock to face the stranger. But even as he struggled to raise himself up he knew it was too late.

As Niall looked up he saw the stranger stagger toward him, one gun drawn. Niall was in a half-crouch up on a knee and one elbow. At least I hit him, thought Niall, as he raised his pistol to meet that of the other man. They were no more than six feet apart — close enough for each to see that the other man's pistol was drawn square on his opponent.

'I watched the front, never thought you'd come over the top.' The stranger's voice was a ragged thing, his breath wheezing. He wasn't standing right.

'You already said that.'

'I was robbed by you.'

'I never robbed a man in my life,' said Niall, his own breath loud.

'You're either forgetful . . . ' — the man swallowed, paused for breath — 'or a liar.'

'Don't listen to him, Niall. He's confused, angry about his brother. That's who's buried here.'

Neither man took his eyes off the other. The sound of Jenna's voice just beyond them in the dark startled Niall. So that was it. The reason for all this. The man wanted revenge for his brother's death. It was so long ago, and just another death of many during that bloody damn range war. Drift had shot the man protecting Jenna, right here in this cave. And now it had come full circle.

The man continued speaking as if she wasn't there. 'How does it feel to have everything taken from you?'

'I don't know yet,' said Niall. The pain in his arm flowered into a numbness that spread across his upper back and chest. 'You should know better,' Niall continued, louder than he intended. The roar of the guns in such a small, enclosed place made them all speak louder than normal. 'A man doesn't have to act like this. He has a choice.'

'You think I had a choice starvin' on my own? Could be my definition of right and wrong is different than yours.'

Niall shook his head now, not taking his eyes from the man's face. 'No. There's right and there's wrong and by the time a fella's grown to a man he should know the difference and live as close as he can to that line.' Niall struggled to keep his voice from wavering. He was so angry with this young idiot. All the death that had happened then and here he was on some fool's errand to try to make it right.

'Easy for you to say,' said the stranger. 'But then you didn't do your growin' in a prison. And besides, you ain't been so successful at it, have you?'

Niall stared at him for a moment, digesting the accusation, then said, 'Maybe not, but I try. Every day, by God, I try.'

'Fella once told me that if you're tryin' then you ain't doin'. Then he beat me for not poundin' rocks fast enough.' There was a pause where the only sound was his ragged, uneven breathing. 'I was fifteen.'

'Don't do this. Don't make me shoot,' said Niall and, as he said it, he seemed to recall saying the same thing to a few men through the years. And he could remember none of their faces.

The man's laugh became a cough and he spit on the floor.

'I remember when your brother died,' said Niall, saying anything to buy time.

'I knew it was you who done it!' The man's voice cracked as he shouted.

'He wasn't a bad man. He wouldn't have wanted this.'

'That's not true, Niall. You weren't even here.'

'Quiet, Jenna!'

'No, he deserves to know the truth.'

The stranger faltered then for a moment, unsure where to point the pistol. 'What truth?' he said, half to the darkness hiding Jenna from them.

Niall heard a muffled crunching sound, like boots on gravel, and then, 'I killed your brother.'

'Jenna, no!'

The stranger growled in frustration and waved his pistol back and forth between Niall and the dark where Jenna was hidden.

'Somebody better make sense,' he said, regaining control, his breathing more ragged than ever.

'Jenna,' said Niall, shaking his head. 'Drift killed him. He told me so.'

'Drift came too late, honey. I made him promise never to tell you. We were the only ones who knew. I'm sorry, Niall, but it's the truth.' He heard the huskiness in her voice and he knew she was crying.

'Why? Why'd you kill my brother?' The man was tired and angry now.

There was no answer. The man shouted, 'Why?' The word echoed louder than all the bullets before it had.

'This was where we had camped. You remember, Niall? You, me, and Uncle Drift? I got trapped out at the ranch that day and we were forced to head up here. Keep moving and fight, you said, and they wouldn't get us.'

'Jenna, it's all right now — '

'No! You were wrong, Niall. They found us. When you and Drift were both away from here. That man got to me. He must have been watching the whole time. As soon as you two left, he came here. And you were gone for so long, Niall. Drift came back first. But by then it was all over with.'

'Jenna, I — '

'Shut your mouth and let her finish!' The stranger's pistol shook with his rage.

Niall heard his wife sniffing in the dark. What was happening here? He didn't understand this at all. He kept his eyes on the stranger, waiting for the slightest moment when he could shoot. To kill.

'He attacked me. Said I was his for the taking. Said I was better than any old piece of land. And then he took me.'

'You killed him!' said the stranger.

'He was so caught up in what he was doing he didn't think I could do

270

anything. I used his own gun.' Her tone had gone flat, cold, functional. 'It was within my reach.'

Silence filled the cave. The three people not even daring to breathe too loudly for fear of being the one to break the complete silence.

Niall's mind sifted the story. It couldn't be true. Uncle Drift did it. He told me so. And he'd never in all my life lied to me. The stranger's hoarse voice, quiet now, broke his thoughts.

'You didn't even have the courtesy to put his name on the grave.'

'We didn't know it,' said Niall.

The stranger's voice rose, his breathing came faster, and he said, 'How could you not know the name of the man whose life you stole? You kill that many men, Winters, that you just forget somethin' like that?' He leaned forward into the shaft of light angling in from the cave's entrance. Niall saw his face clearly now. He was a young man with the tired, angry eyes of someone who has outlived his will to live.

The stranger aimed his pistol at Niall's face and from out of the dark a rock half the size of a man's head slammed into the stranger's face. It all happened as if slowed down, and for the rest of his days Niall remembered the fraction of a second when surprise replaced anger in the young man's eyes. They were looking right into Niall's when Niall pulled the trigger and the man collapsed to the floor of the cave. Niall had seen that softening of the eyes too many times to be mistaken. The man was dead.

22

For a time, neither Niall or Jenna moved. The gunsmoke drifted heavy in the air, curling and unsure. And their heads were full of that peculiar sensation one gets on having just walked away from pounding, rushing water, the body saying that quiet is not yet possible.

Then all at once they each thought of the other. Niall called her name even as he struggled to his feet, pushing himself forward into the dark. And after all this time there she was, in his arms. 'Are you all right?' he chanted in her ear, squeezing her tight and feeling at the same time for any sign that might tell him otherwise.

She leaned into him. 'I am now.'

He carried her to the front of the cave, stepping over the stranger, kicking the man's pistol as he walked. He sat her by the little fire and looked on her for the first time in what seemed like years. They smiled at each other and then she said, 'Niall.'

'Yes?' he still smiled.

'Please untie me.'

'I'm so sorry!' He pulled out his pocket knife and sliced off the rough hemp bindings. Her wrists were raw and bleeding. His ailments were nothing now and he kissed her wrists lightly. He pulled her wadded shawl out from inside his coat and draped it about her shoulders.

'Niall, my shawl. Where did you — ?'

'I found it. On the trail.'

She studied him for a moment and then smiled. He prodded the fire, breathing life into it, and she noticed the blackened tear on his coat's shoulder. He looked at it and said, 'Just nicked me. I'm fine.'

'Take your coat off so I can see it.'

'In a bit. I have to get this fire going first.' He laid on more wood, liberal with it, knowing that even though dark would soon approach, they wouldn't be staying here for the night. Then he rose stiffly, his right foot now hurting him, and though he tried to cover it with a smile, he could see the concern on Jenna's face. 'In a minute, I promise.'

He went through the man's possessions. The saddle-bags offered a variety of useful items, not the least of which was a small wad of grease of some sort. It had a rank odor, he assumed it was cooking grease, but it would do for their wounds until they could get home. Home, he thought. A half-scorched house and a barn with a dead man. He pulled more out of the bags, emptying the contents on the cave floor. Most of the items were food stores, and there was also a lone stick of dynamite. Why on earth would he have such a thing?

A wad of dirty buckskin sat atop two flopped and worn boots. Niall prodded the pile and a little gold chain swayed. He pulled on it and his father's pocket watch appeared. He lifted it free of the dirty garments — they had to belong to

Greasy — and looked at it spinning in the light from the doorway before tucking it away in a vest pocket.

Niall brought the food and grease back to the fire and smeared Jenna's wrists with the powerful-smelling stuff. He filled the coffee pot with snow and in a little while they had a fresh pot of coffee steaming on a flat rock just out of the flames. By then Jenna had tended to his shoulder. The bullet had grazed him, though deeply and painfully, and he was thankful it hadn't been worse. The rest of their ailments would have to wait. The meager food supplies, hard tack and dried meat, along with the scalding hot and strong coffee, went a long way toward reconstituting their strength.

Jenna refused his coat and sweater, so Niall retrieved her fallen wool blanket from the back of the cave and draped it about her. As excited as they were to be together, there was so much that would continue to keep them from talking. Finally, Niall stood and said, 'I should finish things here.' He nodded toward the back of the cave.

There was just enough early afternoon light slanting in for Niall to see the dead man. He felt in the stranger's pockets for something that might tell them who he was, something with a name. But there was nothing other than unused shells for the fairly new twin Colt .45s and nearly forty dollars. Enough for a proper marker for Uncle Drift, he thought. He pocketed the shells and the money, pulled off the gunbelt, retrieved the fallen pistols, and tossed them, holstered, along with the machete, by the entrance near the rest of the man's gear. He would keep what was good, leave the rest, and not feel one whit of guilt over it.

Jenna went outside and stood in the snow overlooking the little canyon. Niall watched her a moment, then dragged the man to the rear of the cave and laid him out beside his brother's grave. He looked down at them for a moment, but couldn't see much. One dead and young, grown twisted and stunted in some ways. The other, older but no less gnarled by life. Niall picked rocks from the brother's grave and piled them on the young man's body. Enough for now, he thought. He let out a deep breath and turned away.

Jenna didn't look at him when he came up behind her. They stood for a moment regarding the pristine scene below.

'Did he tell you his name?' said Niall.

She shook her head, pulled her blanket tighter. 'He never said.'

'Those brothers were more alike than they knew,' said Niall. And as soon as he said it he wished he hadn't.

'Not quite,' she said.

'Jenna, I'm sorry — ' But he didn't know what more to say.

'No,' she said finally, shaking her head. 'I'm the one who's sorry. I never meant to lie to you so long ago. Uncle Drift wanted to tell you the truth, and I did, too, but he was afraid that you might be angry with me and I was afraid you might be angry with him because he left me alone. He was worried about you, said he just wanted to check on you, that he'd be back soon. So we convinced each other to just keep it between us. He said sometimes the truth wasn't worth the pain it would cause. We each made the other promise not to tell you.'

She turned to him and looked up at his tired face. 'Niall, I just wanted to forget everything that happened. And then this.' She gestured limply at the cave and shook her head. 'I'm so sorry we lied to you, sorry we didn't trust in you enough to tell you the truth. Please don't be hard on Uncle Drift. He loves you so.' She looked so thin, so tired. And still so very beautiful to him. He wrapped his arms around her and hugged her close. After a long time she tensed and said, 'Niall, how is Drift? He took a nasty knock. He was unconscious when we left him.'

Niall stroked her hair and held her tight and said nothing. She turned her face away. She knew. They stood there for a long time that way. He would have to tell her all of it soon enough. But the weight of knowing was enough for now.

23

It was another half-hour before they threaded their way on horseback down through the little snowed-in canyon. Niall rode Slate and trailed the dead man's horse. Jenna rode Sweet Baby and towed the docile old pony with a lead line, thankful that she now had free use of her hands. The late afternoon sun raised bright colors off the softening surface of the snowy landscape. Branches and rocky overhangs dripped steadily and as he looked back Niall saw rivulets on the cliff face increasing in strength with each passing minute as the sun melted the snow on the craggy peaks above.

Niall had found the horses about where he thought they would be, huddled and sullen and tethered to rope lashed among rocks in a cleft well below the foot trail to the cave. He split the last of the man's meager corn rations among the four beasts and saddled his and Jenna's horses, and left the roan and the pony bare. He tossed Greasy's decrepit old saddle into the cave.

After an hour of slow going, Jenna's horse shied and cut wide around something to the side of the trail. Nothing but lumps in the snow. Jenna looked down as they passed the spot but Niall urged her on. 'Who can say what's in a horse's mind,' he said, sounding more like Drift than ever, she thought.

And shortly thereafter they came upon Mackie, to the right of the trail and just where Niall had left him tied. He nickered and snorted. Niall tied Mackie behind the roan. As Jenna watched Niall's straight back barely sway in the saddle, she noted how different one man could be from another. It was a person's choices in life that caused those differences. She felt that despite their hardships, they had made decent choices. Oh, maybe not the best every time, but more often than not they hit it right. The trouble lay in knowing at the time the difference between right and wrong. Sometimes it was a mighty thin line that separated the two.

In another couple of hours they drew within sight of the little gypsy wagon, wispy smoke rising from a pipe on the roof, and saw someone breaking branches in the snow beside it. 'Niall,' said Jenna, 'who is that?'

'I forgot to tell you. These are some friends I made on my way up here.'

'What?'

He laughed and as they drew closer to the wagon he waved, then shouted a greeting. The person, a woman, watched for a moment, then waved and shouted, 'Hello!'

As they pulled up and dismounted, the old woman, now smiling, waded through the snow to the pony and hugged it tight around the neck and nuzzled its face with hers. 'Pishka! Oh

Pishka!' she repeated, stroking the stout little animal's chin. Niall noticed something under the wagon wrapped in what looked like an old dress. Their dog, Bella.

'How is your husband feeling?'

'Much better, I thank you.'

Jenna cleared her throat and Niall took his hat off and introduced the two women. While they became acquainted, Niall tethered the animals and found a small stream nearby where he watered the horses well and then fed them from the small supply of corn the gypsies carried for their pony.

The gypsy man's condition had indeed improved. He leant against pillows in the corner of their little bed. The wagon was warm inside and the little stove offered a comforting glow. It was close with four people, but no one seemed to mind. They split what food they had and between Jenna and the old woman, a tasty meal soon appeared. After they ate, Niall recounted the events of the past two days, each person filling in details as they wished.

He hesitated a moment, then explained how he found Greasy. They were all quiet, then the old woman said something in her own language and made as if to spit. The old man patted her arm and she held his hand and said nothing more. Niall continued with his story, explaining his snowshoe trek up the back of the mountain.

'Snowshoes?' said Jenna. 'Where did you get snowshoes?'

'That's the odd part of it. Greasy had turned the place upside down looking for whatever he could carry, and there they were, on the bedroom floor.'

'I know,' said Jenna, with a frown. 'They were your anniversary present.'

'Well thank you very much,' he said. 'I figured as much, after a while, that is. They work well. Unfortunately I won't see them again until I get up there during a thaw. I sort of left them up on the mountaintop.'

'What?' said Jenna. And so Niall continued his tale to the end.

During a lull in the conversation, as Jenna refilled coffee cups, she asked, 'Is the house in very bad shape?'

'It would be much badder,' said the old woman before Niall could reply, and she pointed at her husband, nodding.

The old man looked to the wall and waved a hand at them. 'Ah,' he said, 'It was the storm that put it out.'

'It would have been all gone but for him,' said his wife, her hands waving in the air beside her head like birds. She spoke in such a resolute tone that Niall and Jenna found themselves sitting up a bit straighter.

'I don't know how to thank you,' said Niall. 'You saved our home, our barn.'

'But not the uncle of yours,' the old man said, and again they all grew quiet.

Jenna wiped her eyes and stood up. 'I could use a little night air,' she said, her hands on her back, stretching.

'Gah!' said the old woman, standing so suddenly they all flinched. 'I should have seen before. I am not myself.' She put one hand on Jenna's back, one on her belly, and said, 'But of course you know already. I'm so happy for you.'

'I don't understand,' said Jenna, looking from the old woman to Niall. Niall just shook his head. From behind the old woman they heard a quiet chuckle that grew a little louder.

The old woman smacked her hands together and said, 'Oh, but you do not know yet!' And she hugged Jenna and said, 'But you are to have babies, of course!'

Jenna and Niall just stared at each other. 'How . . . how do you know?' said Niall, staring at his wife's belly.

'I know things,' she said, tapping her long bony nose with an equally bony finger. 'I know.' She nodded in such a way that they could not doubt her.

⋆   ⋆   ⋆

Before it grew dark, Niall went outside to check the horses. Jenna followed and helped him to rub each animal with a bit of sacking. 'Niall, I'd like for them to stay with us.'

'So would I, but that's up to them. He's in no shape to travel and they don't have much.' He rubbed Mackie's shoulder.

'How are you feeling?' he asked, hugging her.

'I don't know. Fine, I guess.' In a moment she said, 'You're going to — '

'Go back, yes. I have to. It's the only way we can put this behind us forever.' The thought of Greasy's body curled up and naked on the trail was too much for Niall to bear, no matter the terror he caused in his final days, Greasy deserved a burial of some sort, if only so that Niall wouldn't think on cold evenings for years to come what he should have done for a fellow man. 'I will not carry guilt,' he said. He stepped back, still holding her arms, and said, 'And besides, we have more reason than ever to make sure it's ended now.'

She just nodded. 'When?'

'In the morning. You head toward

home. I'll be back with you before you get there. I'll take Slate. He's rested more than Mackie. You'll have to head the wagon train.' He smiled. 'Just stay on the old trail. From here it leads right smack dab between the house and the barn. If you get worried, just keep a sharp eye for the slashed tree trunks.'

★   ★   ★

Well before the sky filled with light the little camp was ready for travel. Niall had twitched the wagon out of its rut with Slate and Mackie. The old woman drove the wagon, her dog bundled at her feet, and the stranger's horse and Mackie tied trailing behind. Jenna rode lead on Sweet Baby, and Niall rode with them out of the little clearing and onto the old trail. Now that the snow was melting, the going was easier and the direction was visible enough.

As he rode from them, Niall was thankful that this was only the first snow of the season. Most of it would soon melt off and with any luck they might have a few more weeks of decent weather before winter settled in. He hoped there would be enough time to repair the fire damage to the house and barn. But the first and most important thing they would attend to would be to bury Uncle Drift. As soon as I get back, he vowed.

He reached back into the saddle bag and felt for the stick of dynamite. The cave would hold nothing more than bad memories and the remains of three misguided men.

His thoughts turned from the men to Drift to the wagon he left in the barn. It seemed like a lifetime ago. In some ways it was. He smiled. Jenna was sure going to like that spinning wheel.

THE END

We do hope that you have enjoyed reading this large print book.

Did you know that all of our titles are available for purchase?

We publish a wide range of high quality large print books including:
Romances, Mysteries, Classics
General Fiction
Non Fiction and Westerns

Special interest titles available in large print are:
The Little Oxford Dictionary
Music Book, Song Book
Hymn Book, Service Book

Also available from us courtesy of Oxford University Press:
Young Readers' Dictionary
(large print edition)
Young Readers' Thesaurus
(large print edition)

For further information or a free brochure, please contact us at:
Ulverscroft Large Print Books Ltd.,
The Green, Bradgate Road, Anstey,
Leicester, LE7 7FU, England.
Tel: (00 44) **0116 236 4325**
Fax: (00 44) **0116 234 0205**

Other titles in the
Linford Western Library:

REMEMBER KETCHELL

Nick Benjamin

The brutal beating from big cattle boss Ethan Amador left cowhand Floyd Ketchell near death: punishment for daring to fall in love with his beautiful daughter, Tara. Now, returning five years later, and a top gunfighter, he wants his revenge. But he finds many changes in the town of Liberty, Texas. Tara, a ranch boss herself, has a handsome hard-case as her right-hand man. Can Ketchell rekindle the fierce passion they had once shared and still kill her father?

MASSACRE AT BLUFF POINT

I. J. Parnham

Ethan Craig has only just started working for Sam Pringle's outfit when Ansel Stark's bandits bushwhack the men at Bluff Point. Ethan's new colleagues are gunned down in cold blood and he vows revenge. But Ethan's manhunt never gets underway — Sheriff Henry Fisher arrests him and he's accused of being a member of the very gang he'd sworn to track down! With nobody believing his innocence and a ruthless bandit to catch, can Ethan ever hope to succeed?

DEATH AT BETHESDA FALLS

Ross Morton

Jim Thorp did not relish this visit to Bethesda Falls. His old sweetheart Anna worked there and he was hunting her brother Clyde, the foreman of the M-bar-W ranch. Her brother is due to wed Ellen, the rancher's daughter. He is also poisoning the old man to hasten the inheritance. Thorp's presence in town starts the downward slide into violence . . . and danger for Anna, Ellen and Thorp himself. It is destined to end in violence and death.

VENGEANCE UNBOUND

Henry Christopher

There are some folk who brand Russell Dane a coward — some believe him to be a murderer. And Dane has many more who want him dead: the man he should have fought in a duel; his own uncle; the town that tried to lynch him, and the outlaws he takes refuge with. With so many out for his blood Dane must learn to handle a Colt and confront his enemies. Will his gun craft keep him alive . . . ?

SHOOT-OUT AT OWL CREEK

Corba Sunman

With a law star in his pocket and a gun in his holster, Kell Bannon rides into the Big Bend country of Texas to set up the Parfitt gang for capture. Prepared for a shoot-out, he faces more trouble with Clarkville's crooked Sheriff Bixby; the aggressive ranch foreman, Piercey; and Mack Jex, boss of the local rustling business. It's tough work, and for Bannon, he knows that only his deadly gun and quick shooting can bring a satisfactory result.